學生英語

拔尖寫作

TIP-TOP

English Writing

Chau Lam Ho
(Michael)

責任編輯　黃家麗
裝幀設計　趙穎珊
排　　版　肖　霞
印　　務　龍寶祺

學生英語拔尖寫作 Tip-top English Writing

作　　者　周林浩 Chau Lam Ho (Michael)
出　　版　商務印書館（香港）有限公司
香港筲箕灣耀興道 3 號東滙廣場 8 樓
http://www.commercialpress.com.hk
發　　行　香港聯合書刊物流有限公司
香港新界荃灣德士古道 220-248 號荃灣工業中心 16 樓
印　　刷　嘉昱有限公司
香港九龍新蒲崗大有街 26-28 號天虹大廈 7 字樓
版　　次　2025 年 7 月第 1 版第 1 次印刷

ISBN 978 962 07 0660 8
Printed in Hong Kong

學生英語
拔尖寫作
TIP-TOP
English Writing

Chau Lam Ho
(Michael)

商務印書館

目錄 Contents

範文目錄
Sample Writing of Different Text Types

前言 Introduction

本書針對高小及初中學生的需要編寫，內容包括常用體裁如日記、網誌、私人電郵、建議信、故事、看圖作文等，詳細分析每種體裁的結構、組成部份，由淺入深，一步步引導讀者豐富寫作內容，提高寫作技巧。

每種體裁均提供英文範文，清晰標示各項學習重點、延伸知識以及該體裁的常用詞彙及句式，方便掌握，並有助讀者應付校內及校外的英文寫作評估。此外，也針對香港學生詞彙不足的問題，提供表示不同心情的常用詞彙及表達方式，如表達「開心」，讀者可能只懂用 happy，其實也可以用其他近義詞如 delighted、joyful 和 thrilled；此外，也可以用更生動的表達方式，如 scream with joy、give each other a fist pump 和 give a high five。除了詞彙之外，更附中英對照實用例句，有助讀者掌握這些情感詞彙，日後可以用英語描述不同的心情。

本書作者周林浩 Chau Lam Ho (Michael) 香港大學一級榮譽畢業，在香港高級程度會考英國語文科考獲 A 級（作文亦為 A 級），香港中學文憑考試英國語文科考獲 DSE 5**（作文 Paper 2 Part A 滿分），並於教師語文基準試考獲作文滿分。周老師公開試成績卓越，以其豐富的英語教學經驗，為讀者提供優質內容及學習方法，幫助讀者考取更美滿的成績。

商務印書館編輯部

考考你 Do you know?

你對英文寫作有多少認識？對不同體裁和風格有深入的了解嗎？
嘗試回答以下問題，測試自己對不同體裁的認識，再考慮這本書是否適合你閱讀吧！

1. 寫日記時，最後一段除了寫出事件的結果之外，還可以寫甚麼讓你的日記更發人深省？

2. 寫網誌時，可以用縮略語（e.g. If you're interested...）或簡寫（e.g. Leave a comment below asap and ten of you will win a flight ticket to HK.）嗎？

3. 寫建議信給朋友時，可用甚麼詞彙對朋友遇到的困難表達同情呢？

4. 寫故事時，應用甚麼時態（tense）呢？

5. 寫正式書信給校長 Ms Wong Shuk Man 時，上款應寫 Dear Ms Wong Shuk Man 還是 Dear Ms Wong 呢？

6. 給政府官員 Mr Wong Tai Man 發邀請函時，應用 With love 、 Yours sincerely 還是 Yours faithfully 作為祝頌語呢？

7. 寫投訴信時，我們或許對產品或服務感到十分不滿，可用甚麼詞彙強烈但不失禮貌地提出解決問題的建議呢？

8. 寫影評時，可以描述電影的細節、結局或評論演員的演出嗎？

9. 寫計劃書時，可用甚麼詞彙禮貌地提出建議或表達意見呢？

10. 寫演辭時，可以怎樣在開首喚起聽眾對主題的興趣呢？

答案：

1. 寫日記時，最後一段除了寫出事件結果外，還可以寫出你的**反思** (reflection)，可以是你的感想或從此事裏汲取的教訓。例如，若你記錄同學考試作弊被發現的經過，可在最後一段寫自己從此事中學會必須在考試前作好充份準備，並且在考試時嚴格遵守規則，以免因一時僥倖的心態作弊而須承受嚴重後果。這樣，你的日記會更發人深省。

   如欲了解更多寫日記的技巧和注意事項，可參閱本書第 32 至 33 頁。

2. 寫網誌時，應用親切友善的語調，像跟讀者說話一樣。你可使用縮略語 (e.g. you're, I've)，但不應用簡寫 (e.g. HK, ppl, asap)。

   如欲了解更多寫網誌的技巧和注意事項，可參閱本書第 34 至 37 頁。

3. 寫建議信給朋友時，如想對朋友遇到的困難表達同情，可以用下列表達形式：

   It is really **frustrating** that...

   I **can fully understand** how sad you were...

   You're not alone. Many others have the same problem.

   小提示

   frustrating 指令人氣餒、泄氣的。

   如欲參閱更多例子或了解更多寫建議信的技巧和注意事項，可參閱本書第 40 至 45 頁。

4. 寫故事時，應該用**過去式**講述已發生的事。例如：

   David **was** horrified when he **saw** the man with a knife in his hand. 'Let's hide under this table,' he **said**.

   如欲參閱更多例子或了解更多寫故事的技巧和注意事項，可參閱本書第 46 至 48 頁。

5. 本題的答案是 Ms Wong。

   寫正式書信時，上款應用 Ms / Mr / Mrs / Dr 以及收信人的姓氏，不用列出收信人的全名。

   如欲了解更多寫正式書信的技巧和注意事項，可參閱本書第 53 至 54 頁。

6. 本題的答案是 Yours sincerely。

   寫正式書信時，如上款是 Ms / Mr / Mrs / Dr 以及收信人的姓氏（例如 Dear Ms Lee、Dear Dr Wong），祝頌語為 Yours sincerely。如不知道收信人的名稱，例如當上款是 Dear Sir / Madam 或 Dear Customer Services Manager 時，祝頌語為 Yours faithfully。With love 是非正式書信中所用的祝頌語，可以在寫信給親朋好友時用。

   如欲了解更多寫邀請函的技巧和注意事項，可參閱本書第 55 至 56 頁。

7. 寫投訴信時，我們或許對產品或服務感到十分不滿，如欲強烈而不失禮貌地提出解決問題的建議，可以用下列詞彙：

   I **urge** you to...

   I must **ask** you to...

   I **suggest** that you...

   I **demand**...

   如欲了解更多寫投訴信的技巧和注意事項，可以參閱本書第 57 至 63 頁。

8. 寫影評時，不應該透露太多電影細節，更絕不能公開結局，因這樣會令讀者失去到戲院看該齣電影的興趣。你可以評論演員的演出，但切記不要透露電影細節。

如欲了解更多寫影評的技巧和注意事項，可參閱本書第 64 至 68 頁。

9. 寫計劃書時，如欲禮貌地提出建議或表達意見，可以用下列詞彙：

We **propose** / **think** / **believe**...

We would like to **recommend** / **suggest** that...

如欲了解更多寫計劃書的技巧和注意事項，可參閱本書第 71 至 74 頁。

10. 寫演辭時，如欲在開首喚起聽眾對主題的興趣，可指出一個令人震驚的事實或以虛構的情境引起聽眾思考。例如，當講及環保主題時，可告訴聽眾每秒鐘約有一個足球場大小的樹林被砍伐，或讓聽眾思考若他們住在堆填區附近會有甚麼感受。例如：

令人震驚的事實

Every year, an average of 28 million hectares of forest are cut down. That's one football field of forest lost every single second around the clock.

虛構的情境

What would you feel if there were a landfill in your neighbourhood? What if there were five in every district of Hong Kong?

如欲了解更多寫演辭的技巧和注意事項，可參閱本書第 81 至 89 頁。

分數分析：

0-4 分：看來你對英文寫作的體裁格式、技巧和用詞認識不深。快以此書作為參考，快速提升你英文寫作的能力吧！

5-8 分：你對英文寫作的體裁格式、技巧和用詞似乎有基本的認識和概念。本書有詳盡解釋，可讓你對不同體裁都有更深入的了解，提升你英文寫作的能力！

9-10 分：你對英文寫作的體裁格式、技巧和用詞認識頗多，但在寫作時會否感到字詞貧乏？本書提供很多實用例子，讓你在寫不同體裁時都能靈活運作，得心應手。

Unit 1

拔尖寫作方法 15 式 On Writing Well

很多香港學生恐懼英文寫作，每當要做英文作文功課時就會感到手足無措。他們主要覺得自己想不到有趣的內容、無法用適當的字詞和句式表達自己的想法、並認為自己在遣詞用句方面都錯漏百出，因而缺乏自信。在本章，我會告訴你十五式，幫助你在寫作前、寫作時和寫作後提升自己的寫作技巧，並增強自信。

✦ 寫作前 ✦

第 1 式：廣泛閱讀

閱讀各種主題和風格的書籍和文章能幫助你理解不同的語言結構和寫作風格。通過接觸各類書籍和文章，你可以掌握不同文體的特點，學習如何組織觀點、擴展內容和運用修辭手法。此外，閱讀能讓你接觸不同的寫作技巧，增強理解力，從而提升表達的清晰度和吸引力。

你可以從自己的興趣開始，選擇適合你的讀物。這可以是報章、雜誌、校刊、故事書、小說、關於天文、地理、歷史、科學的書籍、名人的網誌、電影的網評，或其他吸引你的讀物。

第 2 式：擴充詞彙

定期學習新詞彙和句式，能讓你能用最適合的字詞和句子結構表達你的想法。除了閱讀外，在日常生活中，例如在逛街、看電視和瀏覽社交媒體時，我們都有很多機會接觸到新詞彙。接觸到新詞彙和句式時，多使用網上詞典查找它們的讀音、意思和用法，然後嘗試在寫作和日常生活中運用它們。

很多人會問，我需要把學到的新詞彙和句式抄下來，然後要求自己必須在作文時使用嗎？答案是不需要，因為你抄寫下來的新詞彙和句式，未必最適合表達當前的情況，反而會讓句子看起來生硬奇怪。只要自己有充足的詞彙，並且掌握這些詞彙適合用於哪些情況，寫作時你就會得心應手，找到最適合的字詞，並以最自然的方式表達。

第 3 式：了解寫作主題

清楚審閱寫作主題，確定文章的體裁，了解你為甚麼要寫作 — 是為了記錄事件、提供資訊、表達意見還是有其他目的。這將影響你的寫作方式和語氣。此外，考慮誰會閱讀你的作品，並且根據特定讀者的興趣和程度來調整你的語言和風格。

例如，寫私人電郵給朋友講述轉校後的新生活時，你須描述在新學校的經歷和發表感想，語氣宜親切友善。由於這是非正式文體，可以用縮略語（例如 'I'm' 和 'You'll'），遣詞用字應簡單清晰。寫信給區議員表達如何改善社區環境時，你須就社區現存的問題發表意見，語氣宜禮貌。由於這是正式文體，應避免使用縮略語，詞彙和句子結構亦應保持正式和莊重。

本書仔細解釋不同體裁的特點，並提供大量例子，告訴你面對不同體裁時可使用的各種句式，讓你的行文風格切合不同體裁。

第 4 式：規劃寫作結構

清楚了解主題目的、讀者身份和文體風格後，可以開始規劃寫作結構。例如，寫信給校長表達如何建構環保校園時，文章應該有清晰的邏輯結構，包括引言、主體和結論。在引言中，簡要介紹寫信的目的；在主體部份中，具體闡述校內同學的環保意識，以及目前存在的問題和改進的空間；在結論中，重申對環保校園的期待，並建議具體的措施。這樣的寫作方式不僅能表達你的觀點，還能讓校長感受到你對學校環保工作的真誠關心與重視。

本書清楚闡述不同體裁的結構，示範各部份的特點，讓你寫作時能輕鬆規劃結構。

第 5 式：創建思維導圖

在開始寫作之前，可使用思維導圖等寫作工具，組織零碎的思想，比如將你的主要想法寫在中心，並圍繞中心擴展相關的想法。這種視覺組織工具能幫助你看到想法之間的聯繫並規劃你的寫作，讓你更容易擴展內容。

例如，寫信給校長指出同學的壞習慣會引起環境問題時，你可先創建以下的思維導圖：

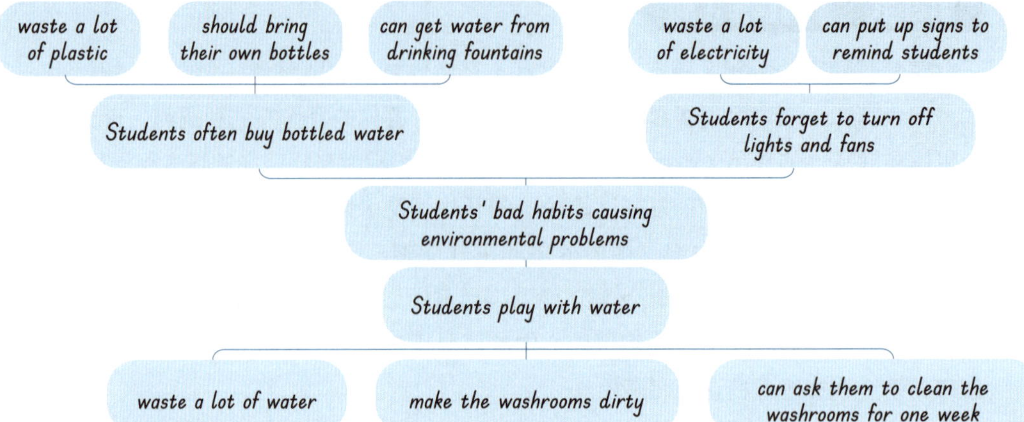

思維導圖有以下好處。

首先，它能幫助你整理和視覺化自己的想法。將同學的壞習慣從中心圖分支出來，這樣你就能清楚看到各個主題之間的聯繫。

其次，思維導圖有助確定重點。透過分層次地排列想法，你可以先指出同學的壞習慣，然後進一步闡述它帶來的環境問題和相應的解決方法，從而使信件內容更加精煉和有條理。此外，你還能確保可以考慮到所有重要的觀點和論據，避免遺漏。

最後，思維導圖有助提高寫作效率。寫作時，你能快速參考思維導圖中的要點，避免在寫作過程中迷失方向，不用重複思考和浪費時間，這樣能更快完成高質量的信件。

總括而言，創建思維導圖不僅能幫助你在寫作過程中組織和表達想法，還能提升寫作的質量和效率，讓你更快更妥善完成寫作。

寫作時

第 6 式：使用主旨句

主旨句通常位於段落開頭，為接下來的內容提供了明確方向，讓讀者能預期所要討論的重點。這種結構使文章更具組織性，增強了邏輯性和流暢性。此外，主旨句還能幫助你保持焦點，避免偏離主題，從而使整體寫作更具說服力和影響力。

閱讀以下例子：

Bullying undermines the self-esteem of its victims. When someone is bullied, they often feel unworthy and lose confidence in themselves. They may start to believe the hurtful things that bullies say. This can make them feel lonely and scared to interact with others. Over time, these feelings may affect how they see themselves and their ability to enjoy life.

在這段中，主旨句 '**Bullying undermines the self-esteem of its victims.**'（欺凌削弱了受害者的自尊心。）的作用是提供整段文字的主要觀點。它清楚表達欺凌對受害者產生的負面影響，讓讀者明白接下來的內容將圍繞這個主題展開。主旨句不僅引導讀者在這個主題上集中注意力，還為後面的細節提供了背景，使整段文字更具連貫性和清晰度。

第 7 式：加入例子和理據

用相關的事實、數據或個人經歷來支持你的觀點。這能為你的寫作增添可信度，並有助吸引讀者。

例如，談及恆常運動可帶來不少好處時，你可以透過以下三個方法豐富你的寫作。

1. 以事實支持：

   Doing regular exercise brings a lot of benefits. It improves your heart functions and increases blood circulation. Regular physical activities also help prevent diseases like diabetes and can improve mental health by reducing anxiety and depression.

2. 以數據支持：

   Doing regular exercise brings a lot of benefits. The World Health Organisation states that working out for at least 150 minutes a week can lower the risk of heart disease by 30 to 40%. Additionally, people who exercise regularly are 50% less likely to develop type 2 diabetes compared to those who don't.

3. 以個人經歷支持：

   Doing regular exercise brings a lot of benefits. I've noticed that jogging boosts my energy and helps me deal with stress better. On days I go jogging, I have a clearer mind at work and better sleep.

   以上方法有效協助你擴展內容，使觀點更可信、更有說服力。

第 8 式：使用連接詞

連接詞能使文章更流暢、結構更清晰。它使文章的內容更連貫，避免突兀的轉折，提升整體可讀性。

在文章結構方面，連接詞能使不同觀點或段落之間的關係明確，便於讀者理解。

在句子結構方面，連接詞能幫助讀者理解句子之間的關係，例如因果或對比，增強內容的邏輯性。使用適當的連接詞亦可以使句子之間過渡得更自然，讓讀者容易跟隨你的思路。某些連接詞亦可以用來強調重點或關鍵觀點，讓讀者注意到文章中的重要信息。

比較以下例句：

1a. Jeffrey is the richest man in his country. He is often depressed.

傑弗里是他國家最富有的人。他常常感到沮喪。

1b. Jeffrey is the richest man in his country. **Nevertheless**, he is often depressed.

傑弗里是他國家最富有的人。儘管如此，他卻常常感到沮喪。

(1b) 句的連接詞 '**Nevertheless**'（儘管如此）表明儘管 Jeffrey 擁有極多財富，但他卻常常感到沮喪，這種矛盾情況更加突出。使用連接詞後，兩種相反情況可以引起讀者思考，為甚麼如此富有的人會感到沮喪，這促使他們進一步探索背後的原因，增加了文章的深度和吸引力。

2a. The soup was too salty while the salad had a strange smell. There was a fly on the steak I ordered.

湯太鹹，沙律有異味，我點的牛排上有一隻蒼蠅。

2b. The soup was too salty while the salad had a strange smell. **What's worse**, there was a fly on the steak I ordered.

湯太鹹，沙律有異味。更糟糕的是，我點的牛排上有一隻蒼蠅。

(2b) 句中，'**What's worse**' 的作用是引入一個更嚴重或更令人不快的情況。它強調了前面提到的問題（湯太鹹和沙律有異味。）之後，還有一個更糟糕的情況，即點了的牛排上有一隻蒼蠅。這個短語不僅讓讀者意識到情況的惡化，還增強了整體的負面印象，讓人感受到不滿和失望。

以上例子示範連接詞如何幫助讀者理解句子之間的關係，讓讀者容易跟隨作者的思路。

第 9 式：使用不同的句子結構

不同的句子結構（如簡單句、複合句和複雜句）可以減少重複的表達，讓文章更具新鮮感，提升讀者的興趣。此外，通過調整句子結構，你可以將重點放在特定的內容上，例如將重要信息放在句首或句尾，增強其影響力。最後，不同的句子結構還有助更精確和生動地表達思想和情感，讓讀者更容易理解和產生共鳴。

比較以下例句：

1a. Wallace noticed a burglar on the balcony. He rushed to his room immediately.

華勒斯注意到陽台上有小偷。他立刻衝回自己的房間。

1b. Noticing a burglar on the balcony, Wallace rushed to his room immediately.

注意到陽台上有小偷，華勒斯立刻衝回自己的房間。

(1a) 由兩個簡單句子組成，而 (1b) 則是一個包含分詞構句 (participial phrase) 的複雜句。(1b) 比 (1a) 更清楚地顯示了因果關係。通過將「注意到」和「衝回房間」放在同一個句子中，讀者能夠立即理解 Wallace 的行動是因為他注意到入侵者，這樣的因果關係更強烈。此外，(1b) 的表達方式強調了 Wallace 的迅速反應，讓讀者感受到他在面對危險時的緊迫感和驚慌，這種語氣的強調使情境更加生動。

2a. You don't want more landfills so you should take action now.

你不想要更多垃圾堆填區，所以你應該現在就採取行動。

2b. You don't want more landfills, do you? Act now!

你不想要更多垃圾堆填區，對吧？立即行動！

在這兩句中，(2b) 比 (2a) 更能有效地傳達緊迫感。(2b) 使用了反問句 'You don't want more landfills, do you?'，這種結構不僅引起讀者的注意，還能促使他們思考自己的立場。這樣的提問方式增加了語句的互動性，讓讀者感到被直接邀請參與討論。此外，(2b) 中的 'Act now!' 直接呼籲立即行動，使語氣更迫切。這種簡潔明瞭的指示讓讀者感受到立即行動的重要性，從而提高了說服力。總結而言，(2b) 利用反問和直接的呼籲，使信息的傳達更生動、緊迫和具說服力，從而更有效地引導讀者的思考和行動。

以上例子示範了不同句子結構如何強調重點和更精確生動地表達思想和情感，從而提升讀者的興趣。

第 10 式：時刻考慮你的讀者

時刻考慮讀者能使你的寫作更具針對性和有效性。了解讀者的需求、興趣和理解能力，使選擇的語氣和語言更符合他們的期望，從而提高信息的傳達效果，增強讀者的共鳴與參與感，最終促進更好的溝通與理解。例如，若你是學生會會長，正準備一份演辭，在開學日時向同學解釋守規矩的重要性，你應該使用輕鬆而親切的語氣，並結合一些校園生活的案例，讓他們明白守規矩的意義與好處。例如，提到遵守校規如何有助於營造更安全的學習環境，你可分享一些成功校友的故事，激勵他們以這些校友為榜樣。這樣的方式不僅能吸引同學的注意，還能讓他們感受到你的誠意與關心，從而更容易接受你的觀點。

✦ 寫作後 ✦

第 11 式：朗讀你的作品

聽到自己的作品可以幫助你發現不地道的措辭、不清晰的句子或文法錯誤，這些在寫作時可能會被忽略。如情況不允許你大聲朗讀（例如你正在考試時），則可在心裏靜靜細讀，也可達致同樣效果。

第 12 式：作出修訂

檢查文法和拼寫錯誤對寫作至關重要，因為這能提升文本的專業性和可信度。錯誤會分散讀者的注意力，影響理解；相反，清晰、正確的表達有助於傳達思想，增強說服力，讓讀者更容易接受和理解內容。你可先自己檢查作品一遍，看看有沒有文法和拼寫錯誤，並作出修訂。現今資訊科技發展迅速，你還可在互聯網上尋找適合你的工具來校對作品，然後進行修改。

第 13 式：尋求反饋

與老師、朋友或家人分享你的寫作，讓他們提供不同視角和建議，幫助你看到寫作中的盲點。其他人的意見能揭示潛在的問題，例如結構不清晰或論點不足，這些往往是你自己難以察覺的。反饋還可以增強信心，讓你了解哪些部份效果良好，哪些部份需要改進。通過與別人討論，你還能更有效地調整語氣和內容，最終提升作品的質量和影響力，達到更有效的溝通目的。

第 14 式：反思寫作過程

透過反思，你能夠明白自己的優點和缺點，了解使用哪些寫作技巧和方法會對作品有益，哪些缺點需要克服。這樣的反思能幫助你改善寫作技巧，增強自信心，避免重複同樣的錯誤，最終提高作品的質量和影響力。同時，反思也能幫助你在未來的寫作中更有效地規劃和組織內容，提高寫作效率和生產力。

第 15 式：欣賞你的努力

花點時間認同自己的努力。完成寫作任務是一項成就，你為此花費了不少時間和心血。你嘗試發表創新的意念和獨到的見解，並運用不同的詞彙和句子結構來表達你的想法。在過程中你不斷思考，還可能需要做大量資料搜集。你的思維開闊了，你的寫作技巧提升了；你進步了，你的寫作能力昇華到另一個層次！因此，你需要欣賞自己的努力，給自己點讚！

記住，你的能力是非常強大的！經過上一次的歷練，你可以嘗試寫作不同的體裁、不同的風格、不同的內容，並為不同的讀者撰寫新的篇章。你做得到！

Unit 2

學習多樣化表達 Different Ways of Saying the Same Thing

使用正確字詞表情達意是寫作的基本功，但如果目標是要爭取達到拔尖水平，就應該多學習一些同義和近義表達形式。本章列出常見的同義和近義詞語及短語，並且提供中英對照的例句。

表達 'happy' 的近義形式 Descriptions related to 'happy'

1.	happy	開心	8.	excited	興奮、激動
2.	pleased/ contented	開心、滿意	9.	joyful/ delighted	高興、快樂
3.	contentedly	滿意地	10.	thrilled	極愉快
4.	relaxed	放鬆、輕鬆自在	11.	ecstatic	狂喜、欣喜若狂
5.	confident	充滿信心	12.	over the moon	非常高興
6.	hopeful	充滿希望	13.	thankful	感恩、感謝
7.	amused	被逗樂、感到好笑			

用說話動作表達 'happy'
When a person feels 'happy', he / she may say...

1.

Chester was **happy** when he got the new scarf. He **said with a big smile on his face**, 'I love this present so much.'

切斯特收到新頸巾時很**開心**，**面上展露燦爛的笑容**。他說：「我非常喜歡這份禮物。」

2.

Ms Helena was **pleased** when she gave the exam papers back to her students. She said **contentedly**, 'You did quite well this time.'

海倫娜老師把試卷交給學生時**很高興**，**滿意地**說：「這次你們做得不錯。」

3.

Aaron was **relaxed** when the bell rang. 'It's great that this semester has ended,' he said.

鐘聲響起時，亞倫感到**輕鬆自在**。「真好，這個學期結束了。」他說。

4.

'I'm sure I will pass my piano exam,' said Uriel **confidently**.

烏列爾**信心十足地**說：「我肯定這次鋼琴考試會及格。」

5.

Leon **looked hopeful** and said, 'Don't worry. The rain will stop soon.'

萊昂**充滿希望地**說：「不用擔心，雨很快會停。」

6.

Anna was **amused**. 'This joke is so funny!' she **laughed**.

安娜被**逗樂**了。「這個笑話真有趣！」她**大笑着說**。

7.

Mike opened the box **excitedly**. He **screamed with joy** and said, 'Wow, I love this pair of sneakers!'

邁克**興奮地**打開盒子，**高興地尖叫着說**：「哇，我很喜歡這雙球鞋！」

8.

Hugo was **joyful** to see his new toy car. He **jumped up and down**. 'Uncle Owen bought it to me from Japan,' he **smiled**.

休戈見到新玩具車後非常**高興**，**蹦蹦跳跳**。「這是歐文叔叔從日本買給我的。」他**笑着說**。

9.

Marcus and Ivan were **delighted** when they saw each other. They **gave each other a fist pump** and said, 'My brother!'

馬庫斯和伊凡見到對方時十分**高興**，他們**互相擊拳**，然後說：「我的好兄弟！」

10.

Curtis was **thrilled**. He **waved his arms** and **cheered**, 'Hurray! Lakers won the NBA championship again!'

柯蒂斯**興奮極了**，**揮動雙臂**，**歡呼道**：「太好了，湖人又贏了 NBA 總冠軍！」

11.

Harris was **ecstatic**. He **held his arms wide** for celebration and yelled, 'We're the champions!'

哈里斯**欣喜若狂**，**高舉雙臂**慶祝，並**大叫**：「我們贏了冠軍！」

12.

Alvin was **over the moon**. He **gave Elvis a high five** and said, 'Yeah! We're going to win again.'

阿爾文**高興極了**，**與埃爾維斯擊掌**，然後說：「喲！我們又會再贏！」

13.

Laura was **thankful**. She **gave Mary a hug** and said, 'I'm grateful for your kindness.'

勞拉很**感恩**，**給了瑪麗一個擁抱**，然後說：「感謝你的慷慨善心。」

表達 'sad' 的近義形式 Descriptions related to 'sad'

1.	unhappy	哀傷、不開心	6.	hopeless	沒希望
2.	sad	傷心、悲哀、令人難過	7.	sorrowful	悲痛
3.	upset	難過、沮喪	8.	desperate	絕望
4.	disappointed	失望	9.	heartbroken	極為傷心、心碎
5.	frustrated	灰心、氣餒			

用說話動作表達 'sad'
When a person is sad, he / she may say...

1.

Cherry was **unhappy**. She **cried**, 'I've lost my favourite pen. It's expensive.'

查爾麗很**不開心**，**哭着說**：「我最喜愛的筆不見了，它很貴的。」

2.

Lily was extremely **sad**. She **sobbed**, 'I've lost my teddy bear. Where's it?'

莉莉非常**難過**。她**抽泣着說**：「我的泰迪熊不見了。到底它在哪裏？」

3.

Sam was **upset**. He **cried**, 'I've lost my phone. Dad bought it to me last week.'

薩姆很**難過**，他**哭着說**：「我的手機不見了。爸爸上星期才買給我的。」

4.

Steven looked at his dictation book **disappointedly** and said, 'I failed my English dictation again. Mum will be very angry. She'll scold me.'

史蒂文**失望地**看着他的默書簿說：「我的英文默書又不及格了。媽媽會很生氣，她會罵我的。」

5.

Ted was **disappointed**. He said, 'I was very nervous in the interview.' Then, he **hid his face in his hands**.

泰德很**失望**。他說：「我在面試裏很緊張。」然後，他**雙手掩臉**。

6.

Ben was **frustrated**. He **wiped his tears** and said, 'I practised so hard but still failed my piano exam.'

賓很**氣餒**，擦去**眼淚**說：「我很努力練習，但鋼琴考試仍不及格。」

7.

'I did so poorly in my violin exam. I'm going to fail again,' said Flora **hope-lessly**.

「我在小提琴考試表現得很差，又會不及格了。」芙蘿拉**絕望地**說。

8.

Gary was **sorrowful**. 'I'll never see Grandpa again,' he **sighed**.

加里**非常悲傷**，**歎息道**：「我再也不會見到爺爺了。」

9.

The old lady looked **desperate** and said, 'He's my only grandson. And now I don't know where he is...' Then, she **burst into tears**.

老婦人顯得**非常絕望**，並說：「他是我唯一的孫兒，但現在我連他在哪裏也不知道⋯⋯」然後，她**哭了起來**。

10.

David was **heartbroken**. He **sat in the corner** and **wept**, 'I'll never see Ivy again.'

大衛**心碎了**，**坐在角落裏哭泣着**說：「我再也不會見到艾維了。」

11.

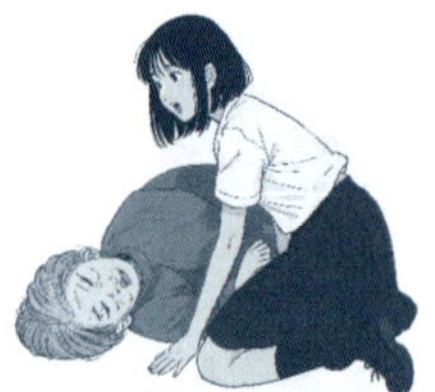

Nicole was **heartbroken**. She knelt next to Grandma, who was lying on the ground, and **wailed**, 'Grandma, wake up!'

妮科爾**難過極了**，跪在躺在地上的婆婆身旁，**號啕大哭**道：「婆婆，快醒過來！」

表達 'angry' 的近義形式 Descriptions related to 'angry'

1. angry 生氣、憤怒
2. annoyed 生氣、煩惱
3. impatient 不耐煩
4. dissatisfied 不滿
5. furious / livid / incensed / irate (= extremely angry) 極其憤怒，大怒

用説話動作表達 'angry'
When a person is angry, he / she may say...

1.

'I don't want to hear that! It's just an excuse!' said Angela **angrily**.

「我不想再聽了，這只是個藉口。」安琪拉**憤怒地**說。

2.

Dave was **annoyed**. He **stomped his feet** and said, 'You're lying. Tell the truth!'

戴夫很**生氣**，**跺着腳**說：「你在說謊。說真話吧！」

3.

Amy said **impatiently**, 'You're late again!''

艾美**不耐煩地**說：「你又遲到了！」

4.

Ms Lee was **dissatisfied**. She **frowned** and said, 'You naughty boy! Why did you forget to bring your homework again?'

李老師很**不滿意**，**皺起眉頭**說：「真是個頑皮的孩子！為甚麼你又忘了帶功課？」

5.

Mum was **furious**. She **stared at** Martin and said, 'I know what happened. Don't lie to me!'

媽媽**非常生氣**，她**瞪着**馬丁說：「我知道發生甚麼事，不要對我說謊！」

6.

Elaine was **furious**. She **pulled her little sister's hair** and **shouted**, 'Don't take my handbag again!'

伊萊恩**氣透了**，她**拉着妹妹的頭髮大喊**：「不要再拿我的手袋！」

7.

Peter was **livid**. He **clenched his fists** and said, 'Stay away from me. You're a liar!'

彼得**勃然大怒**，**緊握着雙拳**說：「離我遠點，你這個騙子！」

8.

Simon was **incensed**. He **slammed the door** and **threw a pillow on the ground**. He then **grabbed Danny by the collar** and **shouted**, 'If you take my phone again, I will slap you in your face!'

西蒙**極其憤怒**，**大力關上門**，**把枕頭掉在地上**，然後**抓着丹尼的衣領大喊**：「如果你再拿我的手機，我會打你一巴掌！」

9.

The zookeeper was **irate**. He **pointed at** Louis and said, 'Don't throw rubbish here! Throw it into the rubbish bin over there!'

動物園管理員**勃然大怒**，**指着**路易說：「不要在這裏掉垃圾！ 掉在那邊的垃圾箱裏吧！」

10.

Ms Au said **sternly**, 'Stop! Don't talk to me like this!'

歐老師**嚴肅地**說：「停！不要這樣跟我說話！」

11.

'Stop making noise. That's not a playground!' **warned** Mum.

「別再吵了，這裏不是遊樂場！」媽媽**警告說**。

12.

'Don't touch the displays. You may break them!' **scolded** the security guard.

「不要碰展品，你可能會弄壞它們！」保安員**責備道**。

13.

Justin **shouted**, 'Don't touch my schoolbag!'

賈斯汀**大喊**：「別碰我的書包！」

14.

'Go away! I don't want to see you again!' **yelled** Tom.

「走開！我不想再見到你！」湯姆**大聲喊道**。

表達 'nervous' 的近義形式 Descriptions related to 'nervous'

1.	nervous	緊張	4.	restless	坐立不安
2.	hesitant / uncertain	猶疑	5.	at a loss	不知所措
3.	anxious / worried / tense / edgy	擔心、不安			

用說話動作表達 'nervous'
When a person feels 'nervous', he / she may say...

1.

'My name is... is Brian and I...' said Brian **nervously**.

「我的名字叫……叫布萊恩，我……」布萊恩**緊張地**說。

2.

Thomas was very **nervous. His heart beat quickly**. 'Will you... will you marry me?' he asked.

湯瑪斯非常**緊張，心跳得很快**。「你……你願意嫁給我嗎？」他問。

3.

'Hmm... I... I'm not sure,' said Carl **hesitantly**.

「嗯……我……我不肯定。」卡爾**猶疑地**說。

4.

'I guess... I guess it's Karen's necklace,' said Tony **hesitantly**.

「我覺得……我覺得這是凱倫的項鍊。」托尼**猶疑地**說。

5.

Ella **said in an uncertain tone**, 'Excuse me. Did you... did you take my umbrella?'

伊拉**一副不肯定的語氣說**：「不好意思，你……你有沒有拿了我的雨傘？」

6.

The waitress looked **anxious** and said, 'I'm... I'm not sure about that...'

侍應生看來有點**不安**，說：「我……我不太肯定……」

7.

William was **worried**. He **clenched his teeth** before the injection and asked, 'Will it be painful?'

威廉很**擔憂**，在**注射前咬緊牙齒**，然後問：「會很痛嗎？」

8.

Matthew was very **tense** as he waited for the interview. He **rubbed his hands** and asked the receptionist, 'Excuse me, when's my turn... my turn for the interview?'

馬修等待面試時非常**緊張**，他一邊**揉擦雙手**，一邊問接待員：「不好意思，請問甚麼時候到我……到我面試呢？」

9.

Diana was **edgy** when she got into the classroom. She **was biting her nails**. Then, she **stammered**, 'Hello, erm... My name... my name is... Diana.'

戴安娜走進課室時感到**緊張不安**，**咬着指甲**，然後**結結巴巴地說**：「你好，嗯……我的名字……我的名字是……戴安娜。」

10.

Oscar was **restless** as he was waiting outside the delivery room. He **kept shaking his legs**. He asked, 'When will I see my baby?'

奧斯卡在產房外等待時**坐立不安**，**雙腿不停抖動**。他問：「甚麼時候才會見到寶寶呢？」

11.

Grandpa was **at a loss**. He **walked a few steps uncertainly** and asked, 'Excuse... excuse me. Where... where is it?'

爺爺**一臉茫然**，**疑惑地走了幾步**，然後問：「不……不好意思，這裏……這裏是甚麼地方？」

表達 'scared' 的近義形式 Descriptions related to 'scared'

1. scared / frightened　害怕、驚恐
2. terrified / horrified　非常害怕、極度驚恐
3. appalled　震驚
4. petrified / aghast　驚呆

用說話動作表達 'scared'
When a person feels 'scared', he / she may say...

1.

Jeremy got **scared**. He **trembled** and said, 'I... I want to go home.'

傑里米**害怕了**，**顫抖**着說：「我……我要回家去。」

2.

Vincent was **frightened**. He **shook** and said, 'I saw a... a big snake!'

文森特很**害怕**，**顫抖着**說：「我看到一條……一條大蛇！」

3.

'I dare not go inside. It's so... so dark,' **said Samuel in a frightened tone**.

「我不敢進去，裏面很……很黑。」塞繆爾**用驚恐的語氣說**。

4.

George was **terrified** and said, 'This dog can... can talk.'

佐治**嚇壞了**，說：「這隻狗能……能說話。」

5.

'There's a big spider!' **yelled** Susan. She was **horrified** and **covered her eyes with her hands**.

「這裏有一隻大蜘蛛！」蘇珊**大叫**。她**害怕極了，用雙手捂住了眼睛**。

6.

Teresa was **horrified** when she saw the man with a knife. She **hid under a desk** immediately and **covered her mouth with her hands**. She thought, 'I can't let that man notice I'm in this room.'

見到拿着刀的男人，特蕾莎**嚇壞了**，立刻**躲在桌子下，雙手掩着嘴巴**。她想：「我不能讓那個男人察覺我在這房間內。」

7.

Bonnie was **appalled** when she went into the kitchen. She asked, 'Why is there so much rubbish on the floor?'

邦妮走進廚房時**嚇壞了**，她問：「為甚麼地上這麼多垃圾？」

8.

Henry was **petrified**. He **trembled** and said, 'The tables and chairs are moving!'

亨利**驚呆了**，**顫抖**着說：「這些桌子和椅子都在動！」

9.

Jasper was **aghast**. He **hid under the blanket** and **shivered**. He **stammered**, 'I saw... I saw a horrible shadow.'

賈斯珀**驚呆了**，**躲在毯子裏瑟縮發抖**，**結結巴巴地說**：「我見到……我見到一個恐怖的黑影。」

10.

'It's getting dark. What... what should we do?' Ryan **asked in a shaky voice**.

「愈來愈黑了，我們應該……應該怎麼辦？」瑞安**一副顫抖的聲線問道**。

11.

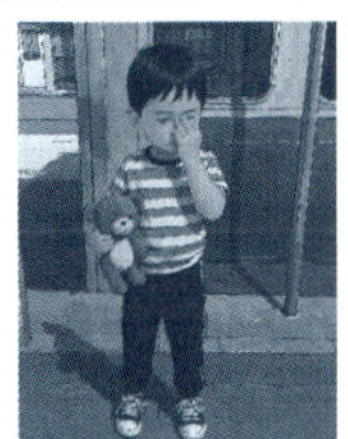

'I'm getting lost. Where is Mum?' **cried** little Tom.

「我迷路了，媽媽在哪裏？」湯姆**哭着說**。

12.

Wilson saw a wolf and **panicked**. He said, 'We have to run!'

威爾遜見到一隻狼，**驚慌失措**。他說：「我們要馬上跑！」

13.

'Please don't... don't hurt us,' **begged** Linda.

「求你不要……不要傷害我們。」琳達**哀求**道。

表達 'bored' 的近義形式 Descriptions related to 'bored'

1.	bored	感到悶或無聊	4.	bored to tears	悶到掉眼淚
2.	uninterested	不感興趣	5.	tired	疲倦
3.	inattentive	漫不經心、不注意	6.	sleepy	倦睏、打瞌睡

用說話動作表達 'bored'
When a person feels 'bored', he / she may say...

1.

Terry felt **very bored**. He **leaned against the wall** and asked, 'When's my turn to kick the ball?'

特里**悶透了**，**倚着牆**問：「甚麼時候才輪到我踢球呢？」

2.

Bruce was **extremely bored**. He **doodled** in his notebook and asked, 'When does this music lesson end?'

布魯斯**悶透了**，在筆記簿上**隨意亂畫**，然後問：「這節音樂課甚麼時候完？」

3.

Carol was **uninterested**. She **rubbed her eyes** and **yawned**, 'Chinese opera is so boring.'

卡羅爾**毫無興趣**，**揉揉雙眼**，**打着呵欠說**：「粵劇真悶啊。」

4.

Eddie looked **totally uninterested** in the toy car. 'Maybe we can play with another toy,' he told Mark.

埃迪看似對那玩具車**完全沒興趣**。「或許我們可以玩其他玩具。」他告訴馬克。

5.

Milton was **inattentive** in the Maths lesson. 'Computer games are much more interesting than Maths,' he said.

米爾頓上數學課時**心不在焉**。「電腦遊戲比數學有趣得多。」他說。

6.

Sarah was **bored to tears**. She **laid her head on the table** and said, 'I hate doing Maths. I want to go home right now.'

薩拉**悶到快掉眼淚，把頭伏在桌子上**說：「我討厭做數學題，真想馬上回家去。」

7.

Grandpa felt **tired** after waiting for three hours. He **slouched** on the armchair and asked, 'When's my turn to see the doctor?'

等了三小時後，爺爺覺得**疲倦**，**無精打采地坐**在扶手椅上問：「甚麼時候才輪到我見醫生？」

8.

Scott felt **sleepy**. He **rested his chin on his hand** and said, 'This video is so boring. I hope it ends soon.'

斯科特感到**眼睏**，**托着下巴**說：「這段影片真悶，我希望它快點完。」

9.

Polly **looked at the clouds** and **daydreamed**, 'If only I could go sunbathing at a beach.'

波利**看着雲片**，**發着白日夢**。她想：「要是我能去海灘曬日光浴就好了。」

10.

Philip **fiddled with his pencil** and said, 'I have no idea about what to draw.'

菲臘**隨意擺弄了鉛筆幾下**，然後說：「我想不到畫甚麼。」

Unit 3

範文舉例 Sample Writing of Different Text Types

3.1 日記 A Diary Entry

寫日記時，寫出一天內發生的特別事情和感想，亦可以加入對話。

日記通常有四部份：

1. 日期和天氣 **(the date and weather)**
2. 開首時簡短描述已發生的特別事情 **(a brief description about the special thing(s) that happened)**
3. 詳細描述已發生的特別事情 **(details about the special thing(s) that happened)**
4. 反思（感想或所汲取的教訓）**(your reflection or how you felt or what lessons you have learnt)**

講述已發生的事情時，記得用過去式。

Examples:

1. I **had** a big breakfast today. **I ate** lobsters and abalones.
   我今天吃了一頓豐盛的早餐。我吃了龍蝦和鮑魚。
2. I **was** late for school. Ms Chan **scolded** me and **punished** me.
   我上學遲到了。陳老師罵我，還懲罰了我。

3.11 範文 Sample writing

1 5th January, 202X Sunny

2 Today was memorable because I witnessed a classmate cheating during the Chinese exam. It started as an ordinary exam. Everyone seemed focused, but then something unusual happened.

簡短描述已發生的特別事情。

3 Halfway through the exam, I noticed something disturbing — my classmate Alex was acting suspiciously. At first, I thought he was just nervous. But then I saw him glancing at his phone under the desk. I was shocked to realise that he was cheating. I wanted to look away, to pretend that I hadn't seen anything, but I couldn't. Then, I thought about giving a signal to him, asking him to stop what he was doing, but I feared that I might disturb others in the exam.

詳細描述當天發生的特別事情，包括你和其他人的感受。

Just as I was wrestling with my thoughts, Ms Yeung walked by. She must have sensed something wrong because she stopped and looked right at Alex. 'Alex, what are you doing?' she asked sharply. His face went pale as he stammered, 'I was just checking...' But he sounded scared. Ms Yeung's disappointment was clear as she asked him to hand over the phone. The whole class was silent, and the tension was thick.

可加入對話，使記敘更真實全面，讓日記看起來更生動。

4 This situation left me feeling uneasy. I understood the serious consequences of cheating but also felt sorry for Alex. He had always been a good student, but he had to face a tough punishment because of a bad choice.

描述一天過後的心情和當天經歷的得着（例如汲取到的經驗或教訓）。

This experience taught me that we need to stick to our principles and not take shortcuts. I realised that having good preparation before exams is important, as it helps us feel confident in our abilities. Additionally, we should always be honest, especially under pressure.

3.12 體裁小測驗 Quiz

1. 日記開首的第一部份是甚麼？

___

2. 可在日記中加入對話嗎？

___

3. 寫日記時，應使用甚麼時態（tense）？

___

4. 日記的最後部份應該寫甚麼？

___

答案：

1. 日期和天氣，例如'21st January, 202X Rainy'。
2. 可以，這樣可讓日記看起來更詳盡和生動。
3. 應使用過去式講述已發生的事情。
4. 日記的最後部份應為「反思」(reflection)，描述一天過後的心情和當天經歷的得着（例如汲取到的經驗或教訓）。

3.2 網誌 A Blog Entry

與寫日記相若，寫網誌時要寫出一天內發生的特別事情和感想。由於網誌可供許多讀者閱讀，可在結尾加入與讀者互動的部份，例如分享感想、向讀者提問題和邀請讀者關注將來的網誌。

網誌通常有五個部份：

1. 網誌名稱 **(the name of the blog)**
2. 標題、作者名稱和日期 **(a title, the writer's name and the date)**
3. 首段簡短描述已發生的特別事情 **(a brief description about the special thing(s) that happened)**
4. 詳細描述已發生的特別事情 **(details about the special thing(s) that happened)**
5. 結尾 **(an ending)**

講述已發生的事情時，記得用過去式。

Examples:

1. We **visited** Macau Tower and **went** bungee jumping.

   我們參觀了澳門旅遊塔，還去了笨豬跳。

2. We **went** to Lord Stow's Bakery and **ate** pork chop buns.

   我們去了安德魯餅店，還吃了豬扒包。

寫網誌時，用親切友善的語調，像跟讀者說話一樣。可使用縮略語 (contractions)，但不應使用簡寫 (abbreviations)。

1. 正確例子 If **you're** a great fan of this blog, you should know that **I've** been to more than 20 outlying islands in Hong Kong. ✓

   如果你是這個網誌的忠實粉絲，你應該知道我去過 20 多個香港的離島。

   錯誤例子 If you are a great fan of this blog, you should know that I have been to more than 20 outlying islands in **HK**. ×

2. 正確例子 Leave a comment below as soon as possible. The first ten people who leave a comment will get a small gift. ✓

   盡快在下面留言吧，最快留言的十個人將獲得一份小禮物。

   錯誤例子 Leave a comment below **asap**. The first ten **ppl** who leave a comment will get a small gift. ×

多樣化語句 Alternative Expressions

開首：
For the beginning of a blog:

a. Hi, everyone. Welcome to today's blog! 大家好！歡迎來到今天的網誌！	**b.** Today, I'm going to talk about... 今天，我要談談……
c. If you've been following this blog for a while, you should know that... 如果你已經關注這個網誌一段時間，你應該知道……	**d.** If you're a great fan of this blog, you should know that... 如果你是這個網誌的忠實粉絲，你應該知道……
e. The moment I've been waiting for a long time has finally come. 我期待已久的時刻終於來了。	**f.** Last time I said that I was going to have a trip to Macau, and this day has finally come. 上次我說要來一趟澳門，這一天終於來了。

結尾：
For the ending of a blog:

a. What do you think about my trip? Share your thoughts in the comments. 你對我這一趟旅程有甚麼看法？在留言中分享你的想法吧。	**b.** What do you think about my experience today? Leave a comment and share your thoughts. 你對我今天的經歷有甚麼看法？留言分享你的想法吧。
c. I hope my experience has taught you that... 希望我的經歷讓您學到……	**d.** I don't know how this will turn out, but I hope that... 我不知道結果會如何，但我希望……
e. If you want to know more about my adventures, pay attention to my updates. I'll be posting about them in the coming weeks. 如果您想知道更多關於我的冒險經歷，請關注我的更新。我將在接下來的幾週發佈相關內容。	

3.21 範文 Sample writing

1 ***Andrew's Travel Blog***

2 **An Interesting Day Trip to Macau**

Submitted by Andrew Chan on 21st May, 202X 9:38 p.m.

3 If you're a great fan of mine, you should know that I was planning a trip to Macau with my parents. This day has finally come and it was a trip with great fun! Let me share with you what we did.

首段簡短描述網誌的主題。

4 Our trip began at Macau Tower, the tallest tower in Macau. We took the lift to the observation deck and enjoyed the beautiful scenery of Macau from there. At more than 200 metres up, the view was a spectacular 360° experience! All the rivers and buildings (including skyscrapers) looked so small. Then, we went bungee jumping. I must say it was the most thrilling moment of my life and I screamed a lot!

After visiting Macau Tower, we went to Lord Stow's Bakery, where we had the famous Portuguese egg tarts and pork chop buns. They were really delicious! The egg tarts were sweet and crispy, while the pork chop buns were fresh and juicy. I had three Portuguese egg tarts and two pork chop buns — they were absolutely the best snacks I've ever had!

詳細描述當天發生的事情。

In the afternoon, we visited the Ruins of St. Paul's. We were amazed to learn that the ruins were actually a wall of a cathedral and that they have remained there since a big fire. We took a lot of photos there.

5 Finally, we went shopping for souvenirs, such as almond cookies and peanut sweets. It was a tiring but unforgettable day. I have learnt a lot about Macau. Have you ever visited Macau? Which place in Macau do you want to visit the most? Leave a comment and tell me what you think.

在結尾描述一天過後的心情和當天經歷的得着（例如汲取到的經驗或教訓）。然後，與讀者互動，例如問讀者問題、邀請讀者留言或關注日後的網誌。

3.22 體裁小測驗 Quiz

1. 網誌的第一部份是甚麼？

2. 寫網誌時，可用縮略語 (contractions) 如 'they've' 嗎？

3. 寫網誌時，應使用簡寫 (abbreviations) 如 'asap' 嗎？

4. 網誌最後部份應該寫甚麼？

答案：

1. 網誌名稱，例如 Tina's World of Fashion。
2. 可以，這樣可讓網誌像跟讀者說話一樣。
3. 不應該。
4. 與讀者互動，例如問讀者問題、邀請讀者留言或留意日後的網誌。

3.3 私人電郵 A Personal Email

在私人電郵中，我們講述日常生活或特別事件，語調宜親切友善。
電郵有七個部份：

1. 收件者的電郵地址 **(the recipient's email address)**
2. 寄件者的電郵地址 **(the sender's email address)**
3. 標題 **(the subject)**
4. 上款 **(a greeting e.g. 'Dear Tom' or 'Hi Peter')**
5. 內文 **(the main body)**
   a. 開首 **(an introduction)**
   b. 內文 **(the matter in detail)**
   c. 結尾 **(a conclusion)**
6. 祝頌語 **(a closing e.g. 'Best regards', 'Best wishes' or 'With love')**
7. 署名 **(the signature line)**

3.31 範文 Sample writing

1	To:	lilychan@hotmail.com	From:	amylee@hotmail.com	2
3	Subject:	My Plan for the Day Trip Next Sunday			

4 Dear Lily,

5 It's great to know that you're coming to Hong Kong for a day trip next Sunday. I'll take you to three places and I hope you'll like them.

Introduction
在開首簡單交代寫電郵的目的。

We'll first visit Ocean Park. There are many aquariums and we can see special marine animals like sharks and jellyfish. We can also go on the mechanical rides and watch Jia Jia and De De, the pandas that recently joined Ocean Park.

Then, we'll go to Ladies' Market. We can buy some clothes and accessories at low prices there. Last month, I bought a beautiful scarf for only 20 dollars there. I'm sure you'll find some good bargains.

Matter in detail
內文

In the evening, we'll go to the Peak. The night view there is amazing. We can watch the lights on the tall buildings on Hong Kong Island from a high point while enjoying our dinner. It'll definitely be a wonderful experience.

Matter in detail
內文

Tell me how you think about my plan. Bye for now.

Conclusion
結尾

6 Best wishes,

7 Amy

私人電郵的語氣親切友善，而且常用縮略語（例如 ：'I'm sure you'll find some good bargains.'），讓人閱讀起來有與親朋好友說話的感覺。電郵可以用 'Bye for now.' 或 'Talk to you later.' 簡單作結。

3.32 體裁小測驗 Quiz

1. 電郵的標題應關於甚麼？

______

2. 寫電郵給朋友 Peter 時，應該用 'Hi Peter' 還是 'Dear Peter' 作為上款？

______

3. 寫私人電郵時，可以用縮略語（contractions），例如 'she's' 嗎？

______

4. 可以用甚麼詞彙或短語作為私人電郵的結尾？

______

答案：

1. 應概括電郵的主要內容，例如 My new school in Canada。
2. 兩者皆可。但請注意，寫正式電郵時，不應用 Hi 作為上款。
3. 可以。私人電郵的語氣親切友善，而且常用縮略語（例如：**I'm** sure **you've** seen this before.），讓人閱讀起來有與親朋好友說話的感覺。
4. 'Bye for now.' 和 'Talk to you later.' 都是私人電郵常見的結尾。

3.4 建議信 A Letter of Advice

建議信是為親朋好友的難題給予重要忠告的非正式書信，語調宜親切友善，並在其中表示同情，給予支持和鼓勵。

建議信有五個部份：

1. 日期 **(the date)**
2. 上款 **(a greeting, e.g. 'Dear Tom')**
3. 內文 **(the main body)**
   a. 開首（概括問題、給予支持和鼓勵）**(an introduction in which you generalise the problem, give support and encouragement)**
   b. 詳細的建議內容 **(details of your advice)**
   c. 結尾（表示希望情況會好轉、給予支持和鼓勵）**(a conclusion in which you express your hope that the situation will improve, give support and encouragement)**
4. 祝頌語 **(a closing)**
5. 簽署及署名 **(the sender's signature and name)**

多樣化語句 Alternative Expressions

開首：
Introduction:

概括問題 Generalise the problem

a. It's true that many Hong Kong students find it difficult to learn English. 確實很多香港學生覺得學習英語很困難。	**b.** I understand it's hard to quit smoking. 我明白戒煙是很難的。
c. It's really unfortunate that your classmates treated you like this. 你被同學這樣對待，真的很不幸。	

給予支持和鼓勵 Give support and encouragement

a. Don't worry. I'm going to give you some advice and I believe it'll work.

別擔心。我會給你一些建議，相信會對你有幫助。

b. I'll tell you what to do. Trust me – the problem won't bother you long.

我會告訴你該怎麼做。相信我 — 這個問題不會困擾你太久。

c. I used to have the same problem. I'll tell you how I dealt with it and I believe you'll no longer find it a problem soon.

我以前也遇過同樣問題。我會告訴你我怎麼處理它，相信你很快就不再覺得這是個問題。

詳細建議內容：
Details of the advice:

具體地指出問題 Identify the problem

a. **I'm sorry to hear that** you spent a lot of time memorising the spellings of the words but you still failed your dictation.

我很遺憾聽到你花了很多時間去記住單詞的拼寫，但默書還是不及格。

b. **You mentioned that** you had copied the words for many times before the dictation but you still failed.

你提到在默書之前，你已經抄寫了單詞很多遍，但還是不及格。

c. **From your letter, I understand that** you tried a lot of methods to quit smoking but you still haven't succeeded.

從你的信中，我明白你嘗試了很多方法來戒煙，但仍然沒有成功。

d. **It seems to me that** once the desire to smoke comes, you cannot resist it.

在我看來，一旦你有吸煙的慾望，就無法抵抗。

e. **What concerns me the most is** what your classmates do to you is indeed an act of bullying.

我最擔心的是，你同學對你所做的事情確實是一種欺凌行為。

f. **One of your problems appears to be that** you are too shy to express your feelings to others.

你其中一個問題似乎是你太害羞，不敢告訴別人你的感受。

表達同情 Express sympathy

a. **It is really frustrating** when he finds that he's got no result for his efforts. 當他發現自己的努力沒有獲得成果時，真的很沮喪。	**b.** **I can fully understand how sad you were** when you realised that this method was not very effective. 我完全理解當你明白到這種方法不是很有效時，你有多麼難過。
c. **I know it's hard** to give up a habit that you've had for years. 我知道要放棄一個持續多年的習慣是很難的。	**d.** **You're not alone.** Many others have the same problem. 你並不孤單。許多人都有相同的問題。
e. **How could they do this?** Why can't they understand your difference? 他們怎能這樣做？為甚麼他們不能理解你的不同？	

給予忠告 Give advice

(i) 使用第二身代名詞 Use the **second-person pronoun** 'you'.

使用 you 給予忠告，如例句 a – e, g 和 i。

(ii) 使用條件句 Use **conditional sentences**.

使用條件句有禮貌地給予勸告，如例句 d 和 g。

(iii) 使用情態動詞 Use **modal verbs**.

使用 can, may, should 和 must 等情態動詞，如例句 a, b, i。

(iv) 使用祈使句 Use **imperative sentences** in order to give direct commands to the reader.

使用祈使句提出直接的命令，如例句 f 和 h。

a. **You can try to** have a pre-dictation in order to make yourself less nervous when the dictation takes place. 你可以先預默一次，讓自己在真正默書時不會那麼緊張。	**b.** **You may consider** using the words in your writing tasks so that you'll be more familiar with them. 你可以考慮在作文中使用這些單詞，這樣你會更熟悉它們。

c. **I suggest that you** learn phonics so that you can know more about the relationship between the spelling and pronunciation of words.

我建議你學習拼音，以便更了解單詞的拼寫和發音之間的關係。

d. **If I were you, I would** ask my parents to give me less pocket money so that I won't have much money to buy snacks.

如果我是你，我會要求父母少給我零用錢，這樣我就沒有太多錢買零食了。

e. **Why don't you** try to find a substitute for cigarettes? I tried this and it worked.

你何不嘗試找一個香煙的替代品呢？我試過這樣做，真的有效。

f. Drink some cold water when the desire to smoke comes.

想抽煙的時候喝點冷水。

g. **If I were in your shoes, I would** report the bullies to the teachers.

如果我是你，我會向老師投訴欺凌你的人。

h. **Don't** tolerate the bullies. Ask your teachers for help.

不要容忍那些欺凌者。向老師尋求幫助。

i. **You shouldn't** tolerate such an evil act because this will make the problem worse.

您不應該容忍這樣的惡行，因為這會讓問題更嚴重。

結尾：
Conclusion:

表示希望情況會好轉 Express your hope that the situation will improve

a. I hope my advice will help you and things will get better.

希望我的建議能幫助你，情況會好起來的。

b. I do hope that you will quit smoking soon.

我真的希望您能盡快戒煙。

c. I really hope that you will have a happy school life.

我真的希望你能有快樂的校園生活。

給予支持和鼓勵 Give support and encouragement

a. Trust me. You'll soon find learning English fun.

相信我，你很快就會發現學習英語的樂趣。

b. I know that quitting smoking is still difficult despite my advice. Whenever you want to give up, write to me. I'll give you more suggestions and I'm always eager to help you.

我知道，儘管有我的忠告，戒煙仍然很困難。每當你想放棄時，寫信給我。我會給你更多建議，而且我總是樂意幫助你的。

c. Remember, whatever the situation is, don't suffer in silence. Be positive and I'm sure that things will work out well. Also, I'll always stand by you.

請記住，無論情況如何，都不要默默忍受。保持積極，我相信事情一定會有好的結果。而且，我會一直支持你。

3.41 範文 Sample writing

1 23rd March, 202X

2 Dear John,

3 I've read your letter and I understand the disappointment of working very hard in English but not getting the results you want. Let me tell you a secret! I was once also uninterested in learning English and never got satisfying results. But don't worry! I'm going to give you some useful tips to improve your English.

Introduction
在信件開首點出問題，給予支持和鼓勵。

You mentioned that you spent two afternoons memorising and copying words every week. I also used to do this but later found that this wasn't a good way to study. Don't you feel bored copying the words repeatedly and forcing yourself to memorise their spelling? I think you should have a new approach! Instead of copying and memorising repeatedly, why don't you try something more fun and interactive? I remember when I studied for dictations, I used to put all the words together and create a story out of them. This helped me understand the meanings of the words. Besides that, I also learnt how to pronounce them properly so that I could try to spell the words based on their pronunciation.

Details of your advice
清楚指出問題所在，表達明白對方的感受，然後用 'I think you should'、'Why don't you' 和 'You may consider' 等詞組給予忠告。

On the other hand, you may consider having a pre-dictation before a dictation — it really works! It will help you get used to the environment and make you less nervous. I always have pre-dictations when preparing for my dictations and they have made me less anxious. Somehow, they have improved my memory as well.

Details of your advice
清楚指出問題所在，表達明白對方的感受，然後用 'I think you should'、'Why don't you' 和 'You may consider' 等詞組給予忠告。

I really hope that my suggestions can help you. Remember, it's important for us to never give up. With hard work and determination, you can make the impossible possible.

Conclusion
在信件結尾再次給予支持和鼓勵。

4 Best wishes,

5 *Max*
Max

3.42 體裁小測驗 Quiz

1. 建議信的內文應怎樣開始？

2. 寫建議信時，可以用甚麼詞彙來指出問題呢？

3. 寫建議信時，可以用甚麼詞彙給予建議？

4. 寫建議信時，內文應該怎樣結束？

答案：

1. 該概括問題，並給予支持和鼓勵。例如，向一位嘗試減肥多次的朋友提出忠告時，可以用下列句子開始：
From your letter, I understand that you've tried several methods to lose weight but failed. Don't worry! I'm going to give you advice that will work.

2. 除了上述例子裏面的'From your letter, I understand that...'之外，還可以用'I'm sorry to hear that...'和'It seems to me that...'等等。

3. 'You can try to...', 'I suggest that you...'和'If I were you, I would...'都是在建議信中用來給予建議的常用詞彙。

4. 給予支持和鼓勵。例如，寫建議信給一位嘗試戒煙的朋友，可以用下列句子結束：
By following my advice, I'm sure that you'll soon quit smoking. Take action now!

3.5 故事 A Story

寫故事時，想出創新意念並加入對話，可讓故事看起來更自然有趣。

故事有四個部份：

1. 開首（例如：描述何時、何地、何人和何事）**orientation (e.g. when and where the story takes place, who the characters are and what happens)**
2. 事件（例如：矛盾或難題）**events (e.g. a conflict or dilemma)**
3. 高潮（故事內最刺激或引人入勝的部份）**climax (the most exciting or intriguing part of the story)**
4. 結尾（交代矛盾或難題如何解決）**resolution (how the conflict or dilemma is resolved)**

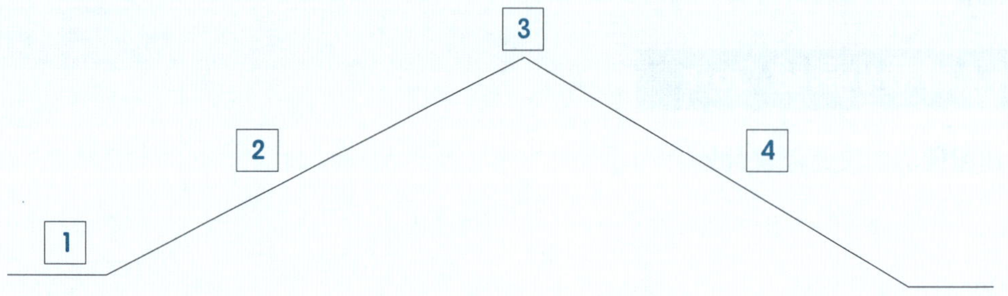

注意講述已發生的事情要用過去式。

Examples:

1. Mum **was** so angry when she **saw** the broken vase.
   媽媽看到破碎的花瓶時非常生氣。
2. 'You're such a naughty boy,' **said** Mum.
   「你真是個頑皮的孩子。」媽媽說。

3.51 範文 Sample writing

1 Today was Peter's birthday. Mum and Dad took Peter to Disneyland to celebrate. Peter was so excited because he was going to see his favourite cartoon character Mickey Mouse.

何時：Peter's birthday
何地：Disneyland
何人：Peter, Mum and Dad
何事：to celebrate Peter's birthday

2 The first place Peter and his parents visited in Disneyland was Hyperspace Mountain. They screamed excitedly on the roller coaster ride. They also rode Dumbo the Flying Elephant, flying high in the air and enjoying the breeze. Peter loved the mechanical rides very much.

Then, Peter and his parents watched a parade and saw many dancers. All the performers had big smiles on their faces and danced energetically. Mum and Dad were impressed by the performers and took many photos.

Suddenly, Mum realised that Peter was lost. 'Where's Peter?' she asked. She looked everywhere but still did not see him.

Peter 走失，難題出現了，故事引入高潮。

3 'Wasn't he standing next to you?' asked Dad. 'Oh, I kept taking photos and didn't look after Peter. It was my fault!' said Dad.

'We have to look for Peter immediately,' said Mum nervously.

Mum and Dad went to different places in Disneyland to search for Peter. They showed other visitors photos of Peter and asked them whether they had seen him. However, no one was able to help. Mum cried, 'Where is Peter? I'm so worried about him.'

故事的高潮，爸爸和媽媽竭盡全力尋找 Peter ，但未能成功，故非常擔心。

4 While Mum was crying, she received a phone call. 'This is from the information centre. Peter is here right now. He got lost,' the helper said. Mum and Dad rushed to the information centre immediately. When they saw him, they hugged him tightly. 'We were so worried about you,' Mum and Dad said.

Peter 被尋回，難題得以解決。

'I'm sorry, Mum and Dad. I saw my favourite cartoon character Mickey Mouse and so I followed him. I will stay next to you and not get lost again,' said Peter. Finally, Peter and his parents continued their trip in Disneyland happily.

3.52 體裁小測驗 Quiz

1. 可以怎樣寫故事開頭？

2. 寫故事時，應該用甚麼時態（tense）呢？

3. 可以怎樣使故事情節更吸引？

4. 可以怎樣寫故事結尾？

答案:

1. 可以簡單描述故事背景，例如時、地、人和事。
2. 寫故事時，應該用過去式講述已發生的事情。
3. 可以為故事創作一個高潮，讓故事看起來更刺激或引人入勝。
4. 應該交代如何解決矛盾或難題。

3.6 看圖作文 A Picture Story

看圖作文時，應該參照寫故事的指引（第 46 頁）。此外，必須仔細描述每幅圖，並且運用想像力創作故事結尾。

首先描述每幅圖內最明顯的人或物，這通常出現在圖的中央位置。然後，描述背景內可見的人或物，以增加細節。

Example:

Last Sunday, Tom and his parents went to a park for a picnic. They brought different kinds of food, such as hot dogs, chocolate cookies, apples and bananas. Tom enjoyed eating hot dogs so much while Mum and Dad loved the beautiful sunshine. It was a nice sunny day. Many birds were flying in the sky and singing in the trees.

可以用以下連接詞組織作文。

有關時間和次序的連接詞 Connectives about time and sequence

First,	Next, / Then, / After that,		Finally,
Firstly,	Secondly,	Thirdly,	Finally,
In the morning,	In the afternoon,		In the evening,
At eight o' clock,	At half past twelve,		At five o'clock,

When they were enjoying their food, a monkey suddenly jumped onto the table.

當他們正在吃食物時，一隻猴子突然跳到桌上。

有關因果的連接詞 Connectives about cause and result

because / since / as 因為

Mum was angry **because / since / as** the monkey took away their fruit.

媽媽很生氣，因為猴子搶去他們的水果。

so / therefore 所以

The monkey took away their fruit, **so** Mum was angry. 或

The monkey took away their fruit. **Therefore**, Mum was angry.

那猴子搶去他們的水果，所以媽媽生氣了。

有關轉折的連接詞 Connectives about contrast

but / however 但是

Dad chased after the monkey **but** it ran very fast. 或

Dad chased after the monkey. **However**, it ran very fast.

爸爸追趕那猴子，但牠跑得很快。

Pictures for Sample writing

3.61 範文 Sample writing

1 Last Sunday, Tom and his parents went to a country park for a picnic. They brought different kinds of food, such as hot dogs, chocolate cookies, apples and bananas. Tom enjoyed eating hot dogs so much while Mum and Dad loved the beautiful sunshine. It was a nice sunny day. Many birds were flying in the sky and singing in the trees.

首先描述圖中最明顯的部份，如郊野公園、人物和桌上的食物。然後，描述背景內可見的事物，如樹和鳥。

2 When Tom and his parents were enjoying their food, a monkey suddenly jumped on the table. Mum was scared. 'Oh no,' she screamed. Dad was shocked as he dropped the bottle of orange juice he was holding on the ground. 'Go away, you naughty little thing,' he shouted. Tom stopped eating immediately and kept looking at the monkey. He couldn't eat because he was shocked by it.

首先描述圖中最明顯的部份：猴子企圖搶走食物。然後運用想像力創作 Tom 和爸爸的想法和說話。

3 Although Dad shouted at the monkey, it didn't go away. Instead, it took an apple and some bananas on the table and ran off. Dad chased the monkey and wanted to get the food back. However, it ran too fast for Dad to follow it. 'You naughty little thing, I must catch you,' shouted Dad angrily.

首先描述圖中最明顯的部份：猴子搶走香蕉，然後爸爸追着牠。然後運用想像力創作爸爸所說的話。

4 Luckily, the monkey tripped on a little stone and fell down, dropping the food that it had stolen. Dad took the food back immediately. Tom went to the monkey and wanted to punch it, but he was stopped by Dad. 'Don't do this, Tom. I'm angry too, but we shouldn't hurt small animals. Now that I've taken the food back, and we should just let the monkey go,' said Dad. 'Maybe the next time we go for a picnic, we shouldn't bring fruit like bananas,' suggested Mum. 'Good idea,' said Tom.

運用想像力創作合理的結局，描述難題如何得以解決。在結局裏，爸爸既取回食物，亦教導 Tom 應愛護動物。

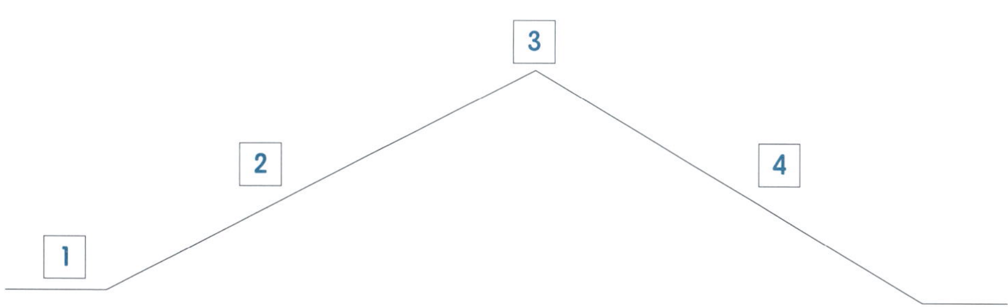

3.62 體裁小測驗 Quiz

1. 看圖作文時，應怎樣描述圖畫？

2. 看圖作文時，可怎樣為故事加入細節？

3. 本單元中提及哪個連接詞有「接着」的意思？

4. 本單元中提及哪個連接詞有「最後」的意思？

答案:

1. 首先描述每幅圖內最明顯的人或物，這通常出現在圖的中央位置。

2. 可描述圖畫背景內的人或物，或運用想像力創作，以增加細節。

3. 'Next'、'Then' 和 'After that' 都有「接着」的意思。

4. 'Finally' 有「最後」的意思。

3.7 公函 A Formal Letter

公函是講述重要事情的正式信件，寫給受尊敬的人，例如校長或區議員。寫公函時，語調必須正式莊重，並且避免使用縮略語（例如：'I'm'、'He's' 和 'She'll'）。

公函有五個部份：

1. 日期 **the date**
2. 上款 **a greeting, e.g. 'Dear Tom'**
3. 內文 **the main body**
   a. 開首 **an introduction**
   b. 內文 **the matter in detail**
   c. 結尾 **a conclusion**
4. 祝頌語 **a closing**
5. 簽署及署名 **the sender's signature and name**

小提示

上款不用列出收件人的全名，只須用 'Mr'、'Ms'、'Mrs'、'Dr' 等稱謂語和收件人的姓氏即可，例如 'Mr Lee'、'Ms Chan' 和 'Dr Lo'。英式英語中，'Mr' 等稱謂語不用加 '.'，這與美式英語的 'Mr.' 等稱謂語有所不同。

小提示

有關祝頌語的用法，寫正式書信時，如上款是 Ms/Mr/Mrs/Dr 以及收信人的姓氏（e.g. 'Dear Ms Lee', 'Dear Dr Wong'），祝頌語為 'Yours sincerely'。如不知道收信人的名稱，例如當上款是 'Dear Sir/Madam' 或 'Dear Customer Services Manager' 時，祝頌語為 'Yours faithfully'。

3.71 範文 Sample writing

1 20th August, 202X

2 Dear Ms Cheung,

3 I am writing to express my concerns about some bad habits of my fellow schoolmates. Those habits have caused environmental problems that are harmful to the Earth. I would like to suggest some solutions.

Firstly, some students buy bottled water at the tuck shop every day and throw away the bottles in rubbish bins. As a result, they waste a lot of plastic. Students should bring their own bottles and fill them with water from drinking fountains. By doing this, they can reduce plastic waste.

Introduction
在開首，以 'I am writing to...' 指出信件的目的，亦可用 'I would like to...' 來指出另一個寫信的目的，例如建議解決方法。

Matter in detail
內文

以 'firstly', 'secondly' 和 'lastly' 簡單分段，然後以主旨句點出每段主旨。

Secondly, some students forget to turn off the lights and fans before leaving a classroom. This wastes a lot of electricity. The school can put up signs on walls to remind students to turn off all electrical devices when leaving a room. By doing this, we can save electricity.

Lastly, some students play with water after washing their hands in the washroom. As a result, they waste a lot of water and make the washrooms dirty. I suggest that the school ask students who play with water to clean the washrooms for one week. By doing this, students will avoid playing with water and will thus save water.

Matter in detail
內文

All students have the responsibility to develop green habits and protect the environment. I hope my suggestions are useful.

Conclusion
在結尾作簡單總結，亦可再次強調問題的嚴重性或建議的重要性。

4 Yours sincerely,

5 *Andy*

Andy Wong (Class 3D)

小提示

給予建議時，可用 'we should'、'we can' 或 'I suggest' 等詞彙。

3.72 體裁小測驗 Quiz

1. 寫公函時，可以用縮略語 (contractions)，例如 'they'll' 嗎？

3. 寫公函時，可以用甚麼詞彙清楚指出信件的目的？

2. 寫公函給梁先生時，上款應是 'Dear Mr Leung' 還是 'Dear Mr. Leung'？

4. 寫公函時，應用 'Yours sincerely' 還是 'Yours faithfully' 作為祝頌語呢？

答案：

1. 寫公函時，必須避免使用縮略語，語調必須正式莊重。
2. 英式英語為 'Dear Mr Leung'，美式英語則為 'Dear Mr. Leung'。請注意，整篇文章應使用英式英語或美式英語，不應兩者夾雜，以讓行文風格統一。
3. 可用 'I'm writing to...' 清楚指出信件的目的。
4. 如上款是 'Ms / Mr / Mrs / Dr' 以及收信人的姓氏 (例如 'Dear Ms Lee'、'Dear Dr Wong')，祝頌語為 'Yours sincerely'。如不知道收信人的名稱，例如當上款是 'Dear Sir / Madam' 或 'Dear Customer Services Manager' 時，祝頌語為 'Yours faithfully'。

3.8 邀請函 An Invitation Letter

邀請函是邀請人出席正式活動、大型慶祝活動或其他場合的信件，語調通常正式莊重。正式邀請函有以下五個部份：

1. 邀請函寄出的日期 the date the invitation is sent
2. 上款 a greeting (e.g. Dear Ms Leung)
3. 內文 the main body
   a. 邀請出席的場合，例如慈善活動、頒獎典禮 the purpose of the invitation, e.g. a charity event, a prize presentation ceremony
   b. 活動細節，例如日期、時間、地點 details of the event, e.g. date, time, venue
   c. 請求收件者回覆是否出席 asking the recipient to reply / to tell whether he / she will come
   d. 寄件者的聯絡資料 the sender's contact details
4. 祝頌語 a closing
5. 簽署及署名 the sender's signature and name

3.81 範文 Sample writing

1 2nd July, 202X

2 Dear Mr Lee,

3 I am pleased to inform you that you have been selected, from the top 5% of the students in your form, to be placed on the Outstanding Student Honours List for your outstanding academic performance in 202X-202X.

以 'I am pleased to inform you that' 來告知喜訊。這是邀請函的常見開首。

You are cordially invited to attend the Prize Presentation Ceremony, at which you will receive an Honours Certificate on stage. The invitation is also extended to two members of your family so that they can share this proud moment with you.

'You are cordially invited to' 亦是邀請函的常用句。

The Prize Presentation Ceremony will be held on 15th July, 202X (Saturday) at 3:00 p.m. in St. Matthew's Hall at Hong Kong College. Please let us know whether you will attend the ceremony by completing and returning the attached reply slip, by fax or by post, to the General Office by 9th July, 202X.

清楚交代日期、時間和地點。

清楚交代如何回覆是否出席活動。

Should you have any enquiries, please contact Ms Jasmine Lee at 2345 7788. I look forward to seeing you at the Prize Presentation Ceremony.

以 'I look forward to seeing you' 來表達期待見到收件者出席活動。請注意，此處 'seeing' 為動名詞 (gerund)，因為 'to' 是介詞 (preposition)。

4 Yours sincerely,

5 *Jasmine*
Jasmine Lee

3.82 體裁小測驗 Quiz

1. 寫邀請函時，可用甚麼詞彙來傳遞喜訊呢？

2. 寫邀請函時，可用甚麼詞彙來發出邀請呢？

3. 寫邀請函時，可用甚麼詞彙來表達期待見到收件者出席活動？

4. 寫邀請函時，應該用 'Yours sincerely' 還是 'Yours faithfully' 作為祝頌語呢？

答案:

1. 撰寫邀請函時，可用 'I am pleased to inform you that...' 來傳遞喜訊。
2. 可用 'You are cordially invited to...' 發出邀請。
3. 可用 'I am looking forward to seeing you' 來表達期待見到收件者出席活動。
4. 一般為 'Yours sincerely'，因為邀請信的上款一般都是個人化，為 'Ms / Mr / Mrs / Dr' 以及收信人的姓氏（例如 'Dear Ms Lee'、'Dear Dr Wong'）。如上款沒有收信人的名稱（例如 'Dear Student'、'Dear Parent'），則應該用 'Yours faithfully' 為祝頌語。

3.9 投訴信 A Complaint Letter

撰寫投訴信時，除了作出投訴，還要建議解決方法。有時更可以給予警告，以促請相關機構妥善回應投訴。縱使撰寫投訴信時，可能對相關問題極度不滿，但態度仍須正式莊重，切忌不禮貌。

1. 日期 **the date**
2. 上款 **a greeting (e.g. 'Dear Ms Leung')**
3. 內文 **the main body**
   a. 開首 **an introduction**
   b. 詳細投訴內容 **the details of the complaint(s)**
   c. 建議解決方法 **a solution**
   d. 警告（非必要）**the warning(s) (optional)**
   e. 結尾 **a conclusion**
4. 祝頌語 **a closing**
5. 簽署及署名 **the sender's signature and name**

多樣化語句 Alternative Expressions

開首：Introduction:

a. I am writing to complain about / lodge a complaint against...

本人……，故特以此函作出投訴。

b. I am writing to express my strong dissatisfaction with...

本人對……感到強烈不滿。

c. I am writing to inform you that the products we ordered from your company have not been supplied properly.

貴公司未能妥善供應本人所訂購的產品，故特以此函告知 閣下。

d. I am writing to inform you of my dissatisfaction with the food and service at Sunshine Restaurant on 23rd May, 202X.

本人 202X 年 5 月 23 日於陽光餐廳用膳，惟對當天的食物和服務感到不滿，故特以此函告知 閣下。

e. I am writing to you because I had an extremely unhappy experience with the service at your resort hotel on 2nd September, 202X.

本人對 202X 年 9 月 2 日在 貴度假酒店的服務體驗極為不滿，故特以此函告知 閣下。

投訴內容：Details of the complaint(s):

a. On 21st January, 202X, we placed an order with your company for 20 water taps. The consignment arrived yesterday but contained only 12 water taps.

202X 年 1 月 21 日，我們向 貴公司訂購了 20 個水龍頭。該批貨物已於昨天到達，但僅包含 12 個水龍頭。

b. I regret to inform you that some of the products have been damaged / stained / scratched / used.

我很遺憾地通知你部份產品已經損壞 / 污損 / 破損 / 被使用過。

c. After leaving your shop, I found that I had been charged $580 instead of $480.

離開 貴店後，我發現我被收取了 580 元，而不是 480 元。

d. The soup was too salty while the salad had a strange smell. What's worse, there was a fly on the steak I ordered.

湯太鹹，沙律有異味。更糟糕的是，我點的牛排上有一隻蒼蠅。

e. There were a lot of used towels on the floor. Besides, the walls were stained and the lights could not be turned on.

地上有很多用過的毛巾。此外，牆壁有污漬，燈也無法開。

f. We told the waiter about the problems but he said that the food was fine. He also said that we were annoying and disrupting his work.

我們告訴侍應這些問題，但他說食物沒有任何問題。他還說我們很煩，打擾了他的工作。

g. When we asked the manager for assistance, he said he was busy and walked away.

當我們請求經理協助時，他說他很忙，然後直接走開。

建議解決方法：
Solution:

a. We urge you to look into the matter promptly / without any further delay. 我們促請您立即調查此事，不要有任何延遲。	**b.** I expect quality service from you and request that you address this issue with immediate attention. 我期望　貴公司提供優質服務，並請求您立即處理此事。
c. We must ask you to send us the remaining products immediately. 我們必須要求　貴公司立即將餘下的產品寄給我們。	**d.** We would like your company to send us replacements for the damaged water taps. 我們希望　貴公司寄送新水龍頭給我們，以取代已損壞的。
e. I would like a refund of the difference as soon as possible. 我希望　貴公司盡快退還差額。	**f.** I must urge you to take immediate action to improve the sanitation of the changing room and the service of the receptionist. 我必須敦促　貴公司立即採取行動，以改善更衣室的衛生情況和接待員的服務。
g. We suggest that you provide a 10% discount on the invoice. 我們建議您在發票費用上提供 10% 的折扣。	**h.** We demand a written apology for the impolite manner of the manager. 我們要求　貴公司就經理的不禮貌行為以書面形式道歉。
i. I have no choice but to cancel my membership, and I demand a refund of the membership fee. 我別無選擇，只能取消我的會員資格，並要求退還會員費。	

警告：
Warning:

a. Otherwise, we may have to look elsewhere for our supplies.

否則，我們可能不得不尋找其他供應商。

b. Unless we hear from you within the next five days, we will consider cancelling the order.

除非我們在未來五天內收到您的回覆，否則我們會考慮取消訂單。

c. Should you be unable to provide a refund, I will have no choice but to lodge a formal complaint to the Consumer Council.

如果您無法提供退款，我別無選擇，只能向消費者委員會提出正式投訴。

d. If these conditions are not met, I am afraid that we will be forced to take legal action.

如果這些條件無法滿足，我們將不得不採取法律行動。

e. Unless you are able to send us a replacement within the next two weeks, we will be compelled to take legal action.

除非您在未來兩週寄送替代品給我們，否則我們將不得不採取法律行動。

f. If I do not hear from you within the next week, I may consider revealing my experience on travel blogs.

如果我在未來一週收不到您的回覆，我可能考慮在旅遊網誌上公開我的經歷。

g. If no action is taken by your company within the next five days, I will report the incident to local newspapers.

如果 貴公司在未來五天內沒有採取任何行動，我將通知當地報章令此事件曝光。

結尾：
Conclusion:

a. Thank you for your attention to this matter.

感謝您對此事的關注。

b. Should you require any further information, please feel free to contact me at 9876 5432. I look forward to your prompt reply.

如需進一步的資訊，請致電 9876 5432 聯繫本人。我期待您的迅速回覆。

c. Thank you for taking time to review my request.

感謝您撥冗審視我的請求。

講述已發生的事情時，注意要用過去式。

Examples:

1. When we **reached** the reception counter, the receptionist **was listening** to music on her headphones.

   我們到達接待櫃台時，接待員正在用耳機聽音樂。

2. While we **were eating** our food, we **saw** some flies on the wall.

   我們在用餐時，看到牆上有一些蒼蠅。

語調可強硬，但切忌不禮貌。避免情緒化的言語和人身攻擊。

1. 正確例子 The dance instructor was overweight and her physique did not look professional. What's more, she was not able to demonstrate some simple dance movements. ✓

   舞蹈老師過重，她的體型看起來並不專業。更甚者，她無法示範一些簡單的舞蹈動作。 ✓

   錯誤例子 The dance instructor was **as fat as a pig**. She is **definitely the fattest and the most stupid person I have ever seen**. Naturally, she could not even do the simplest moves. ×

   舞蹈老師胖得像豬一樣。她絕對是我見過最胖、最愚蠢的人。自然地，她連最簡單的動作都做不到。 ×

2. 正確例子 The steak seemed to be overcooked while the mushroom soup was too salty. ✓

   牛排似乎煮得過熟，而蘑菇湯則過鹹。 ✓

   錯誤例子 The steak **tasted like a stone** while the mushroom soup **was surely the most awful food in the world. Even dogs would not want to eat such food.** ×

   牛排的口感像石頭一樣，而蘑菇湯肯定是世界上最糟糕的食物。相信連狗也不想吃這些食物。 ×

3.91 範文 Sample writing

1 3rd August, 202X

2 Dear Manager,

3 I am writing to formally complain about the fitness dance class FD 123 that I recently joined. I am particularly dissatisfied with the conditions of the changing room, the behaviour of the receptionist and the quality of the dance instructor. Below are the details of my concerns.

Introduction
開首

在投訴信開端，清楚指出投訴事項。

My first lesson of the fitness dance class FD 123 took place at 8 p.m. on 1st August, 202X. When I entered the changing room, I was shocked by its poor sanitary conditions. There were used towels scattered on the floor, and I noticed black stains on some of the walls. Even worse, all the windows were locked, leaving the room poorly ventilated and uncomfortable. When I approached the reception counter for assistance, the receptionist was wearing headphones and listening to music. She completely ignored my request and made no effort to respond.

What disappointed me more was the quality of the dance instructor. The instructor's appearance was unprofessional, as she was overweight and lacked the physical fitness one would expect from a dance teacher. Additionally, she was unable to demonstrate even basic dance movements. For most of the lesson, she played short videos of dance movements and instructed the class to follow them without providing any guidance or feedback. She made no effort to correct students' postures or improve their technique.

清楚指出投訴項目，如購買的產品型號或服務詳情，包括日期、時間和地點等。

Details of complaints
投訴細節

Given my experience, I find the service provided by your studio to be extremely disappointing. I am requesting the cancellation of my membership and a full refund of the class fee. If my request is not met, I will have no choice but to refer this matter to the Consumer Council and local newspapers.

Solution
解決方案

Warning
警告

I look forward to your prompt response. Should you require any further information, please feel free to contact me at 9988 7766.

Conclusion
在結尾留下聯絡資料，讓被投訴的機構容易與你聯絡。

4 Yours sincerely,

5 *Christina*
Christina Lee

3.92 體裁小測驗 Quiz

1. 寫投訴信時，可用甚麼詞彙清楚指出投訴事項？

2. 到一間餐廳用膳後，如你感到食物異常難吃和侍應服務不理想，應該在投訴信中表示 'The food was the most disgusting food in the world and the waiters were very stupid.' 嗎？

3. 寫投訴信時，可以用甚麼語氣強烈但不失禮貌的詞彙，來提出解決問題的建議呢？

4. 寫投訴信時，應在結尾留下你的聯絡資料嗎？

答案：

1. 寫投訴信時，可用 'I am writing to complain about...'、'I am writing to lodge a complaint against...' 或 'I am writing to express my strong dissatisfaction with...' 等詞彙清楚指出投訴事項。
2. 不應該。寫投訴信時，我們或許對產品或服務感到十分不滿，但不應該用不禮貌的詞彙。此情況下，可用 'Both the food and the service of the waiters were not up to standard.' 來表達不滿，語氣雖強烈，但不失禮貌。
3. 可用 'I urge you to...'、'I must ask you to...'、'I suggest that you...' 或 'I demand...' 來提出解決問題的建議，語氣雖強烈，但不失禮貌。
4. 應該留下聯絡資料，讓被投訴的機構容易與你聯絡。

3.10 影評 A Film Review

影評為一齣電影的強項和弱項提供簡短描述，風格可以是正式或非正式的。撰寫影評時，有一點值得留意的是，不應透露太多電影細節，更絕不能公開結局，否則讀者會失去到戲院看該齣電影的興趣。

影評有三個部份：

1. 開首（提供電影的基本資料，例如電影的類型、演員、導演、角色和背景）**an introduction (which gives some background information, such as the type of the film, cast, director, main characters and setting)**
2. 內文（簡短提及情節，並評論演員的演出、導演的技巧和情節；也可評論電影的攝影、剪接、服裝造型設計、動作設計、音樂、音響效果和視覺效果）、**the main body (which briefly introduces the plot and comments on the acting, directing and storyline; as well as the cinematography, editing, costume and makeup design, action choreography, music, sound effects and visual effects)**
3. 總結（提及是否推介電影）**a conclusion (in which you mention whether you recommend the film or not)**

描述電影情節時，注意用現在式。

Examples:

1. Thomas (David Anderson) **is** a farmer who **works** in a remote area in Nottingham.
   湯瑪斯（大衛・安德森）是一位在諾定咸偏遠地區工作的農夫。
2. When he **meets** Sally (Angela Smith), he **falls** in love with her immediately.
   當他遇到莎莉（安琪拉・史密斯）時，立刻愛上了她。

多樣化語句 Alternative Expressions

描述電影背景：About the background of the film:

a. Directed by Raymond Choi, *Diamond Everywhere* is set in... 由蔡端文執導，《無處不在的鑽石》的故事發生於……	**b.** *When He Reaches 30* is based on a novel / the real-life story of a... 《當他三十歲時》改編自一部小說 / 真人真事……

c. Set in 2009, *Brian's Secret* is a comedy / love story / cartoon / action film / horror film / science fiction film / thriller / detective story / kung fu film / war film.

《布萊恩的秘密》以 2009 年為背景，是一部喜劇 / 愛情電影 / 卡通電影 / 動作電影 / 恐怖電影 / 科幻電影 / 驚悚電影 / 偵探故事 / 功夫電影 / 戰爭電影。

描述電影情節：
About the plot:

a. The story begins when...

故事開始時……

b. The story is about...

故事是關於……

c. The situation becomes complicated when...

當……時，情況變得複雜。

d. Things turn bad when...

當……時，情況變差了。

e. However, as it comes close to the date of the competition, Daisy becomes...

然而，當比賽日期臨近，黛西變得……

評論及發表意見：
Comments and opinions:

a. The plot is absolutely touching / romantic / fascinating / exciting / thrilling / inspiring / surprising.

情節非常感人 / 浪漫 / 引人入勝 / 刺激 / 驚心動魄 / 鼓舞人心 / 令人意想不到。

b. However, this part is rather confusing / slow / boring / unconvincing.

然而，這部份相當令人困惑 / 緩慢 / 無聊 / 缺乏說服力。

c. *Warriors* has a large cast and spectacular costumes.

《戰士》擁有龐大的演員陣容和華麗的服裝。

d. Despite her first appearance in a film, Betty Lo shows signs of sophistication in her acting.

儘管是首次演出電影，羅佩蒂的演技已頗成熟。

e. The acting is natural / sophisticated / unnatural / unsophisticated. 演技自然 / 成熟 / 不自然 / 不成熟。	**f.** Although the cast is excellent, the plot is probably too complicated for the audience. 儘管演員陣容出色，但對觀眾來說，劇情可能過於複雜。
g. The music / sound effect matches with the action scenes perfectly. 音樂 / 音效與動作場面完美搭配。	**h.** The theme song is powerful / weak / satisfying. 主題曲強而有力 / 強差人意 / 令人滿意。
i. The special effects are sophisticated / spectacular / superb. 特效精心設計 / 很壯觀 / 精彩絕倫。	**j.** Too many special effects have made the action scenes unconvincing. 太多特效令動作場面缺乏說服力。
k. This part will definitely touch your heart. 這部份一定會觸動你的心靈。	

推介電影：
Recommendations:

a. It is worth watching! 值得一看！	**b.** Don't miss it! 不要錯過這齣電影！
c. I highly / strongly recommend it. 我強烈推薦它。	**d.** This film is highly entertaining / really touching / extremely inspiring. 這齣電影很具娛樂性 / 非常感人 / 極具啟發性。
e. It is worth watching for the visual effects / action scenes / acting of Jimmy Tai alone. 單就視覺效果 / 動作場面 / 戴志明的演技就已經值得一看。	**f.** It will change the way you see street sleepers. 它會改變你對露宿者的看法。
g. The film has succeeded in sending its message to the audience. 電影成功把它的信息傳遞給觀眾。	**h.** It is bound to be a box-office hit. 它一定會成為非常賣座的電影。

i.	Fans of William Lee will no doubt be thrilled with it. 李威廉的粉絲毫無疑問會為電影感到興奮。	**j.**	I would not recommend this film because... 我不會推薦這部電影，因為⋯⋯
k.	The plot is pretty boring / complicated / unconvincing. 劇情相當無聊 / 複雜 / 缺乏說服力。	**l.**	Wait until it comes out on Netflix. 等到它在 Netflix 上映才看。
m.	Only watch this film if you have plenty of time to spare. 當你有很多空閒時間才看這部電影。		

3.101 範文 Sample writing

Released in 202X, *The Soccer Dream* demonstrates how much passion young boys can have for soccer. With a limited budget, Jason Lam produced a film about friendship, which tells how the primary school kids from a soccer team in Tin Shui Wai struggle to fight for their dream — becoming champions in the Hong Kong Inter-school Soccer Competition. Their journey begins when David (Hinson Chan) meets Tim (Benjamin Yau) in the soccer team organised by Mr Fong (Victor Ip). With Mr Fong's special training programme, the team's skills improve by leaps and bounds, helping them secure a place in the Hong Kong Inter-school Soccer Competition.

可在影評的開首指出電影上映年份、導演的名字和電影的類別。

角色的名字後可用括號交代演員的名字。

Winning seems to be an easy job for the boys when they cooperate well and play every match in unity. However, when David and Tim start to compete for the Top Scorer Award, things turn bad. They refuse to pass the ball to each other during matches, and their envy on each other escalates into heated arguments. Despite their first appearance in a film, Hinson Chan and Benjamin Yau demonstrate effectively how passionate young boys can be about soccer and how immature they can become when friendship turns to envy. Without any special directing effects, Jason Lam captures every moment of passion, cohesion and unity within the team, as well as envy and hatred that arise later on.

可在內文評論演員的演技和導演的拍攝技巧。

In spite of a very simple plot and an extremely low budget, the director has succeeded in conveying a very important message to the audience — young and immature as some boys can be, their power can be great when they unite. How will Mr Fong intervene to address the boys' conflict? Will the two boys become friends again? Will they achieve their goal? You can find the answers by watching this inspiring film in the cinema. Don't miss it!

除了 'The film is definitely worth watching!' 等詞彙，可直接呼籲讀者觀賞電影，以表示推介該電影。

3.102 體裁小測驗 Quiz

1. 寫影評時，應該在開首指出電影類別（例如動作電影、驚悚電影）嗎？

____

2. 寫影評時，應該用甚麼時態（tense）來描述電影情節呢？

____

3. 寫影評時，可怎樣交代演員的姓名？

____

4. 寫影評時，可用甚麼詞彙強烈推介電影？

____

答案：

1. 應該，這讓讀者清楚知道電影的類別，從而決定電影是否適合自己觀看。
2. 應該用現在式描述電影情節。
3. 可以在角色名字之後用括號交代演員的姓名。
4. 可用 'Don't miss it!'、'It's worth watching!' 和 'I highly recommend it!' 等句子來強烈推介電影。

3.11 資訊性文章 An Informative Text

資訊性文章為人、動物、地方、機構等提供資訊，一般都有標題。要組織好文章，可加入小標題，然後在下方提供相關資訊。

講述一般性事實時，應使用簡單現在式。

Examples:

1. Lions **are** mammals. They **have** light brown hair.

   獅子是哺乳類動物，有淺棕色的毛髮。

2. Tokyo **is** the capital of Japan. There **are** many tall buildings.

   東京是日本的首都，那裏有許多高樓大廈。

講述歷史事實時，注意使用過去式。

Examples:

1. Albert Einstein **was** born in 1879.

   愛因斯坦出生於 1879 年。

2. The building **collapsed** in 1998.

   該建築物於 1998 年倒塌。

3.111 範文 Sample writing

Koalas

Introduction

Koalas are mammals. They are not bears.

可用小標題組織文章，讓讀者清楚知道每部份講述的內容。

Appearance

Koalas are about 63 to 75 centimetres tall. Their fur is soft, thick, grey and white. They have big ears. They have sharp claws and teeth to help them eat tree bark. They also have pouches like kangaroos.

資訊性文章是正式文體，故須避免使用縮略語。

Habitat

Koalas live on the east coast of Australia. They live and sleep in eucalyptus trees.

Diet

Koalas are herbivores and eat plants. They eat leaves, bark, fruit and flowers. They eat 0.45 kilogram of leaves per day to stay healthy.

Behaviour

Koalas move to a different tree every day. They sleep up to 19 hours a day.

Interesting facts

Koalas are born blind and hairless. Besides, they do not drink water. Instead, they get water from the leaves they eat.

Summary

Koalas are endangered because people cut down eucalyptus trees. If people continue to do so, there will be no places for koalas to live. They will have no food as well.

3.112 體裁小測驗 Quiz

1. 資訊性文章應該有標題嗎？

____

2. 為甚麼在寫資訊性文章時可加入小標題？

____

3. 在資訊性文章講述事實時，應該用甚麼時態（tense）？

____

4. 撰寫資訊性文章時，可用縮略語（contractions），例如 'he's' 嗎？

____

答案:

1. 應該，這可以讓讀者清楚知道文章主題。
2. 這可以讓讀者清楚知道每部份講述的內容。
3. 講述一般性事實時，用現在式。講述歷史事實時，用過去式。例如，'The Great Wall is a famous tourist attraction in China. It was built in the Qin Dynasty.'
4. 資訊性文章是正式文體，故須避免使用縮略語。

3.12 計劃書 A Proposal

計劃書是為機構或個人（例如學生會或校長）提供計劃或建議的正式文章，目的是說服讀者支持當中的計劃或建議。

計劃書有四個部份：

1. 標題 **title**
2. 開首 **introduction**
3. 建議 **recommendations**
4. 總結 **conclusion**

計劃書的行文正式而簡潔。

Examples:

1. In this proposal, we will address...

   在這份計劃書，我們將探討……

2. We would like to suggest...

   我們建議……

3. The solution to this is...

   解決方案是……

給予建議、表達觀點和陳述事實時，用簡單現在式。此外，代表機構寫計劃書時，應該用 'we' 代替 'I'。

Examples:

1. We believe that a talent show is a good idea because most parents and students like watching performances.

   我們認為才藝表演是個好主意，因為大多數家長和學生都喜歡觀賞表演。

2. As most students are keen on sports competitions, we believe that an inter-class badminton competition is a good idea.

   由於大多數學生熱衷於體育比賽，我們認為舉辦班際羽毛球比賽是個好主意。

給予建議時，亦可用被動句。

Examples:

1. A fun fair could be held at the covered playground.

   可以在有蓋操場舉辦同樂日。

2. Game stalls could be set up by different school clubs.

   各個學校社團可以設置遊戲攤位。

講述不同情況時，可以用條件句。

Examples:

1. If it rains, the match can be held at the sports centre.

   如果下雨，比賽可在體育中心進行。

2. The event can be held on Friday if the school hall is not occupied.

   如果學校禮堂沒有人使用，活動可以在星期五舉行。

多樣化語句 Alternative Expressions

開首：Introduction:

a. The Sport Association was asked to give recommendations on... 體育協會將就……提供建議。	**b.** After extensive discussion with the members, we... 與會員進行廣泛討論後，我們……
c. We will discuss the advantages and disadvantages of... in this proposal. 我們將在本計劃書討論……的利弊。	**d.** We would like to bring forward a proposal for... 我們將在此計劃書建議……

表達意見：Proposing ideas:

a. It seems to us that... 我們認為……	**b.** We propose / think / believe... 我們提議 / 認為 / 相信……
c. We recommend / suggest... 我們建議……	

總結：Conclusion:

a. We hope this proposal meets with your approval. 我們希望這份計劃書能獲得您的批准。	**b.** We would appreciate it if you could consider the suggestions accordingly. 如果您能考慮相應的建議，我們將不勝感激。

3.121 範文 Sample writing

1 **Proposal for Activities on Open Day**

2 **Introduction**

The Student Union was asked to recommend activities that could be carried out on the Open Day. We would like to make the following suggestions.

在開首清楚指出計劃書的目的。

3 **Recommendations**

(a) School Tour

To let visitors know more about our school, we suggest organising a school tour. Students can serve as tour guides who bring visitors to different special rooms and let them experience what the lessons in the rooms are like. We believe that visitors would be particularly interested in special rooms such as the STEM room and the music studio.

在建議的部份加入小標題，可讓讀者清楚知道每項建議的主題。此外，每段以主旨句先作交代，然後給予詳細內容。

(b) Talent Show

A talent show could be held at the school hall. In the talent show, students could form groups to sing, dance or give other performances on stage together. We believe that the show would give students a chance to showcase their talents. If we have enough budget, we could invite a pop singer to perform with students together, which would add excitement to the talent show.

(c) Fun Fair

A fun fair could be held at the covered playground. Game stalls could be set up by different school clubs and run by students. Small gifts could be given to visitors after they play the games. In addition, food stalls could be set up, and students could sell snacks and soft drinks to visitors.

4 **Conclusion**

We hope that our proposal will be put forward. We would appreciate it if you could provide feedback. Thank you for your consideration.

在總結裏，禮貌地請求讀者採納建議和給予意見。

3.122 體裁小測驗 Quiz

1. 代表機構寫計劃書時，應該用 'I' 還是 'we'？

2. 在計劃書給予建議、表達觀點和陳述事實時，應該用甚麼時態（tense）？

3. 寫計劃書時，可以用甚麼詞彙禮貌地提出建議或表達意見呢？

4. 寫計劃書時，可以用縮略語（contractions），如 'he's' 嗎？

答案:

1. 應該用 'we'。
2. 應該用現在式。例如，'As most students are interested in music performances, we believe that a charity concert is a good idea.'
3. 可以用 'We propose that...'、'We believe that...' 或 'We would like to recommend that...' 等詞彙提出建議或表達意見。
4. 計劃書是正式文體，故須避免使用縮略語。

3.13 意見調查報告 A Survey Report

意見調查報告需客觀陳述和總結調查結果，必須用正式語調並注意以下幾點：

- 不使用縮略語。**Do not use contractions.**

  E.g. did not ✓ didn't ×

- 使用正式的主語。**Use formal subjects.**

  E.g. The survey asked... 調查詢問……✓

  I asked... 我詢問…… ×

- 使用被動句。**Use the passive voice.**

  E.g. A survey was conducted... ✓ 進行了一項調查……

  I conducted a survey... × 我進行了一項調查……

- 使用複述句。**Use reported speech.**

  E.g. The survey asks whether students have a hobby. 該調查詢問學生是否有愛好。✓

  Do you have a hobby? 你有愛好嗎？ ×

意見調查報告有四個部份：

1. 標題 **title**
2. 開首 **introduction**
3. 調查結果 **survey results**
4. 總結 **conclusion**

報告調查結果時，可以用確實數字。

E.g. Forty of us like English a lot. Only two of us do not like it.

我們當中有四十人非常喜歡英語，只有兩個人不喜歡。

亦可用以下詞彙概括數據。

- all (全部)
- the majority (大部份) most (多數)
- not many (不是很多)
- few (少數)
- none (全無)
- about one third (大概三分之一)
- more than four fifths / more than 80% (超過五分之四 / 超過 80%)
- less than one quarter / less than 25% (少於四分之一 / 少於 25%)

Findings of the Favourite Subject of 1B Students

Total number of students: 39

Subject	Number of students who like the subject	Number of students who find the subject easy
Chinese	26	26
English	31	12
Mathematics	21	10
Physical Education	39	37

3.131 範文 Sample writing

1 **Survey Report on the Favourite Subject of 1B Students**

2 **Introduction**

A survey on the favourite subject of 1B students was conducted in an English lesson yesterday. 39 students were asked whether they liked four particular subjects, namely Chinese, English, Mathematics and Physical Education. They were also asked whether they found the subjects easy or difficult.

在開首指出意見調查的問題、對象和人數。

3 **Survey Results**

The survey results show that all students liked Physical Education. In addition, all but two students reported that they found this subject easy.

描述調查結果時，可先描述數字較大的項目，然後順數字由大至小描述其他項目。

Coming in second is English, with slightly more than 75% of the students reporting that they liked it, although only slightly more than 20% of the students reported that they found this subject easy. Regarding Chinese, two thirds of the students said that they liked this subject. The same number of students reported that they found the subject easy.

Mathematics is the least favoured subject as only slightly more than half of the students said that they liked it. On the other hand, only ten students found the subject easy.

4 Conclusion

The survey results show that the favourite subject among 1B students is Physical Education, with the greatest number of students finding it easy. On the other hand, the least popular subject is Mathematics and only ten students found it easy.

在總結中，可簡略重提數字最大和最小的兩項。

3.132 體裁小測驗 Quiz

1. 寫意見調查報告時，可以用縮略語（contractions），例如 'they've' 嗎？

2. 意見調查報告的首段應該寫甚麼？

3. 在報告你問了甚麼問題時，應該用 'I asked...' 還是 'The survey asked...'？

4. 在報告數字時，應該用確實數字還是大概數字？

答案：

1. 意見調查報告是正式文體，故須避免使用縮略語。
2. 應該指出意見調查的問題、對象和人數。
3. 應該用 'The survey asked...'。
4. 兩者皆可。

3.14 議論文 An Argumentative Essay

議論文為爭議性議題表明立場，並以理據和分析作支持。

1. 開首（概括議題、提供背景資料和陳述立場）an introduction **(which outlines the topic, provides the background information and states the stance)**
2. 內文（提供理據支持你的立場和反駁反方意見）the main body **(which provides reasons that support the stance and rebut opposing ideas)**
3. 總結（重申立場和總結論點）**a conclusion (which restates the stance and summarises the arguments)**

不要在總結中提出新論點，而要牽動讀者的情緒。**(Do not present new arguments in the conclusion. Rather, appeal to readers' emotions.)**

你可用以下方式表明立場：

1. **I am of the opinion that** our school should build a new library instead of a new swimming pool.
   我認為本校應興建新圖書館，而非新游泳池。

2. **In my opinion,** secondary school students should wear a school uniform.
   我認為中學生應該穿校服。

3. **Although** exams are **undesirable** for most students, they are **necessary**.
   雖然考試對大多數學生來說是不受歡迎的，但卻是必要的。

4. **Although** allowing students to bring their phone to the classroom **may seem to be an interesting idea**, it indeed **generates a lot of problems**.
   儘管允許學生帶手機進課室看起來是個好主意，但實際上會引起很多問題。

5. When we consider carefully, we will know that **the disadvantages** of online lessons **far outweigh the benefits**.
   當我們仔細考慮時，就會知道網課的缺點遠遠超過其好處。

3.141 範文 Sample writing

1 **Heritage Preservation: A Blessing Rather Than a Curse**

標題清晰表明立場。如表達某議題弊大於利，可用 'A curse rather than a blessing'。

Owing to economic development, we can see more and more skyscrapers. To make space for these tall buildings, it seems inevitable that some old historic buildings have to be demolished. However, many people still try to protect these historic buildings. In my opinion, these historic buildings should be preserved because of their important value.

在開首提供背景資料，指出爭議出現的原因。然後，可用 'In my opinion' 或 'I am of the opinion that' 來表明立場。

2 First of all, heritage preservation helps promote Hong Kong's attractiveness to tourists. Instead of visiting beautiful beaches or going shopping in huge malls, many tourists nowadays like visiting places of educational value in order to broaden their horizons. For example, the Arch of Triumph in France attracts many tourists every day. The historic buildings of Hong Kong can also serve as tourist attractions and help generate significant revenue for Hong Kong's tourism.

以簡單的主旨句點出段落的中心思想，然後擴展。

In addition, heritage preservation can enrich culture. Some historic buildings represent the collective memories of Hong Kong people. They are a record of what life was like in the past. Protecting them helps enhance Hong Kong people's sense of belonging.

提供最少兩個理據以支持你的立場。

Some people may argue that historic buildings are too short and should be replaced by tall buildings so as to provide more space for residential and commercial use. However, for the development of a sustainable city, economic growth and heritage preservation should be balanced. In fact, our economy can benefit from heritage preservation because of the revenue from tourism.

指出反方意見，然後反駁。

3 To conclude, heritage preservation helps promote tourism and increase Hong Kong people's sense of belonging. Its benefits far outweigh its harms. It is important to preserve buildings of great historic value.

在結尾重申立場和總結論點，可用 'To conclude' 或 'In conclusion' 作總結。可以比較議題的好處和壞處（或優點和缺點），說明作出取態的原因。如指出優點比缺點多，亦可以用 'Its merits outweigh its shortcomings.'

3.142 體裁小測驗 Quiz

1. 寫議論文時，可以用甚麼詞彙清楚表達立場？

____

2. 在議論文的內文中，可以怎樣清楚指出每段的中心思想？

____

3. 應該在議論文中反駁反方的意見嗎？

____

4. 本單元提及那兩個詞彙可以用來總結論點？

____

答案：

1. 寫議論文時，可以用 'In my opinion, ...' 或 'I am of the opinion that...' 來表明立場。
2. 可以用簡單的主旨句點出段落的中心思想。
3. 絕對應該，這可以令你的文章更具說服力。
4. 'To conclude, ...' 和 'In conclusion, ...' 都可以用來作總結。

3.15 演辭 A Speech

演辭是特別場合中為聽眾演講時準備的講稿。在演講中，講者為主題提供資訊或表達個人意見。

演辭有四個部份：

1. 問候語 **a greeting**
2. 開首（點出主題、提供背景資料並且引起聽眾興趣）**an introduction (in which you introduce the topic, provide the background information and arouse the interest of the audience)**
3. 內文（探討議題，並以實例、證據、個人經歷等支持自己的觀點）**the main body (in which you address the issue and support your ideas with illustrations, evidence, anecdotes and so on)**
4. 結尾（總結觀點和提及難忘的事情，並且讓觀眾反思）**an ending (in which you wrap up the topic and leave something memorable for the audience to think about)**

問候語 The greeting

演講開始之前，首先向觀眾致意。慣常做法是先提及嘉賓和要員。

1. Sir Marcus Davidson, Professor Lee, Fellow Members of the European Studies Society, Ladies and Gentlemen, ...

   馬庫斯・戴維森爵士、李教授、各位歐洲研究學會的會員、先生、女士們，……
2. Dear Principal, teachers and fellow students, ...

   校長、各位老師、各位同學，……

開首 The introduction

開首除了簡短告訴聽眾演講的內容，還要喚起他們對主題的興趣。你可用以下方法：

1. 直接陳述（如主題本身已頗有趣）**A direct statement (if the topic is inherently interesting)**

   E.g. Today I'm going to tell you how to get good grades in exams without having to study a lot.

   今天我將告訴你們如何在考試中取得好成績，而不需要花很多時間學習。
2. 問題（以引起觀眾思考）**A question (to stimulate thinking)**

   E.g. How many plastic bags on average do you use when you go grocery shopping? Do you use more than five plastic bags?

   當你去購物時，平均會用多少個膠袋？你用超過五個膠袋嗎？

3. **反問句（以表達立場或意見）A rhetorical question (to take a stand or voice an opinion)**

E.g. Nowadays, some parents still use corporal punishment as a way of parenting. Don't you think this is unacceptable? How can the society tolerate this?

現在，一些父母仍然使用體罰作為教養孩子的方式。你不覺得這是不可接受的嗎？社會怎麼能容忍這種行為？

4. **令人震驚的事實 A shocking fact**

E.g. Every year, an average of 28 million hectares of forest are cut down. That's one football field of forest lost every single second around the clock.

每年，平均有 2,800 萬公頃的樹林被砍伐，這意味着平均每秒就有一個足球場大小的樹林被砍伐。

5. **軼事 An anecdote**

E.g. Last Saturday, I had my badminton practice as usual. I saw a ten-year-old kid who played with powerful strokes and nimble footwork. After training, the kid invited me for a match. As a veteran badminton player with more than ten years of experience, I lost the match unexpectedly. That made me review my training routines and think about how my training can be more effective.

上星期六，我像往常一樣練習羽毛球。我看到一個十歲的小孩，打球有力且步伐靈活。練完球後，那小孩邀請我打一場球。出乎我意料之外，作為一個有十多年羽毛球經驗的老球手，我意外地輸掉了比賽。這讓我重新檢視了我的訓練計劃，並思考如何提高訓練成效。

6. **虛構的情境 An imaginary situation**

E.g. What would you feel if there were a landfill in your neighbourhood? What if there were five in every district of Hong Kong?

如果你住的地方附近有一個垃圾堆填區，您會有甚麼感受？如果香港每區都有五個堆填區呢？

7. **名人格言 A quote of a famous person**

E.g. In his inaugural address, US President John Kennedy said, 'Ask not what your country can do for you — ask what you can do for your country.'

美國總統約翰・甘迺迪在就職演說中說：「不要問國家能為你做甚麼 — 要問你能為國家做甚麼。」

內文 The body

在內文，以理據、例子、數據和個人經歷等實例支持自己的觀點。

1. 理據 Evidence

Not drinking enough water brings a lot of problems to our health. **Various medical reports show that it leads to headaches, fatigue, moodiness, dry skin and an increased risk of strokes.**

喝不夠水會對我們的健康帶來很多問題。各種醫學報告顯示，這會導致頭痛、疲勞、情緒不穩、皮膚乾燥和中風風險增加。

2. 例子 Examples

Many NBA players had a better career path after they changed teams. **For example, Kevin Garnett won his first and only NBA championship title a year after he changed his team.**

許多 NBA 球員在轉換球隊之後，都有更好的職業生涯。例如，凱文・加內特在換隊一年後贏得了他的第一個，也是唯一的 NBA 冠軍頭銜。

3. 數據 Figures

Teenagers are facing more and more pressure at school nowadays. **A recent study by the University of Hong Kong revealed that more than 20% of teenagers in Hong Kong have considered committing suicide because of the pressure at school.**

現今青少年在學校面臨越來越多的壓力。香港大學最近的一項研究顯示，超過 20% 的香港青少年曾因學業壓力而考慮自殺。

4. 個人經歷 Personal experiences

My health has improved a lot after I developed the habit of exercising every day. **Now, I have better sleep, feel more energetic, have a clearer mind at work and have less stress.**

在我培養每天運動的習慣後，健康得到很大改善。現在，我睡得比以前好，精力更充沛，工作時頭腦更清晰，壓力也減少了。

結尾 The ending

演講的結尾與開首同樣重要，它通常是聽眾印象最深刻的部份，能讓聽眾記住它。你可以用以下的方法：

1. **展望將來 A vision of the future**

   E.g. So just now I shared about how to get good grades in exams without spending a lot of time studying. Try these methods and I believe you'll no longer fail your exams!

   剛才我分享了如何在不花費大量時間學習的情況下，在考試中取得好成績。試試這些方法吧，相信你不會再考試不及格了！

2. **行動號召 A call to action**

   E.g. So next time when you go shopping, bring your own bag. It's easy and you'll not only save a few plastic bags, but also make the world a better place to live.

   下次購物時，請自備購物袋。這很簡單，而且你不僅會節省一些膠袋，還會讓世界變成更美好、更宜居的地方。

3. **啟發性的問題 A provocative question**

   E.g. Think about these questions. What is the purpose of parenting? Is it to let kids know the consequences of their behaviour or stop the nuisance brought by kids abruptly? Do you want to stop some problems of your kids right now but bring more problems to them in the future?

   想一想這些問題。教養孩子的目的是甚麼？是讓孩子知道自己行為的後果，還是要立即制止孩子帶來的滋擾？你是否想現在制止孩子的某些問題，但卻為他們將來帶來更多問題？

4. **真實的成功故事 A true story of success**

   E.g. Residents in a town in Switzerland adopted the 3R's I just mentioned collectively and succeeded in reducing the amount of solid waste by more than half. Because of this, the government of the town decided to abandon the plan to build a landfill in the neighbourhood. With the 3R's, we can also reduce waste and landfills.

   瑞士一個小鎮的居民集體採用了我剛才提到的 3R 方法，成功將固體廢物的數量減少了一半以上。正因如此，鎮政府決定放棄在鄰近地區興建堆填區的計劃。透過 3R 方法，我們也可以減少廢物和堆填區的數量。

最後，向聽眾或觀眾致意。

1. Thank you for being a wonderful audience. I hope this speech gave you something to take away.

   感謝你們這羣出色的聽眾，希望這次演講能讓你有所收穫。

2. Thank you for lending me your time. I hope you'll have some insights after hearing my speech.
感謝你們抽時間聆聽，希望你們聽完我演講後能獲得一些啟發。

3. May I wish you all a good day. Thank you.
祝大家有愉快的一天，謝謝。

4. I wish you every success in the future. Thank you for listening.
祝各位未來一切順利，感謝你的聆聽。

5. I wish you the best of luck in today's events.
祝你們在今天的活動中一切順利。

演辭用語 The language of speech writing

寫演辭時，盡量用簡單的字詞和句子。艱深的字詞可能令聽眾感到困惑；同樣，冗長複雜的句子亦會使人困惑。

1. After the man had a deep inhalation, he expectorated. ×
那個男人深呼吸一口氣後，他吐出了唾液。

   After the man took a deep breath, he spat. ✓
   那個男人深呼吸後便吐了痰。

2. Developing the habit of doing regular exercise is conducive to your physical well-being, boosts your level of confidence and enhances your level of contentment. ×
培養定期運動的習慣有助於你的身體健康，提升你的自信心，並增強你的滿足感。

   Regular exercise is good for your health. Also, it boosts your confidence and makes you happier. ✓
   定期運動有益健康。此外，它還能增強你的自信心，讓你更快樂。

使用不同的句子結構亦是重要的，因此，雖然必須避免使用大量複雜句子，偶然用一兩句較長的句子並無不妥。

演辭最終會被口語傳遞，因此所用的句子都應該簡短和口語化。你可以採用以下手法：

1. 祈使句 **Imperatives**

   E.g. Act now! Don't hesitate!

   立即行動！不要猶豫！

2. 縮略語 **Contractions**

   E.g. Soon, **you'll** know about the awful experiences **he's** come across.

   很快，你就會知道他所遇到的可怕經歷。

3. 插入語 **Parenthetical phrases**

   E.g. You know, ... As we can see, ...

   你知道……正如我們所見……

4. 問題（疑問句或反問句）**Questions (direct or rhetorical)**

   E.g. What does that mean? 這是甚麼意思？（*Direct question 疑問句*）

   Isn't that ridiculous? 這不是很可笑嗎？（*Rhetorical question 反問句*）

5. 人稱代名詞 **Personal pronouns**

   E.g. **We** need your support. Join **us** now.

   我們需要你的支持。立即加入我們。

6. 主動語態（而非被動語態）**Active voice (instead of passive voice)**

   E.g. They wasted more than 50 water bottles and 100 pieces of paper!

   他們浪費了 50 多個水瓶和 100 多張紙！

7. 過渡性的字詞或句子 **Transitional phrases or sentences**

   E.g. **So here's the lesson** — nothing good happens after midnight.

   這就是教訓 — 午夜後不會發生任何好事。

8. 不完整的句子 **Incomplete sentences**

   E.g. Just a click on the mouse. Then, a lot of pictures on the screen.

   只要點一下滑鼠。然後，屏幕上就會出現很多圖片。

以下每一組句子中，其中一句比較口語化。嘗試分辨哪些是看起來更口語化的字詞或句子結構。

1a) We should all help reduce air pollution and turn off idling car engines.
1b) Be responsible citizens. Turn off idling car engines.

2a) Why do teenagers use Facebook? Do they simply want to keep in touch with their friends or do they simply want to kill time? 2b) Why do you think teenagers use Facebook? To keep in touch with friends? Or simply to kill time?
3a) I would now like to talk about the harmful effects of drug abuse. 3b) Now, let me tell you the harmful effects of drug abuse.
4a) You see, we all suffer from air pollution in the end. 4b) In the end, it is the polluters who suffer from air pollution.

1b, 2b, 3b, 4a 是看起來比較口語化的句子結構。

具說服力的演辭能引起聽眾的興趣和啟發他們。你可用以下技巧讓演講聽起來更具說服力。

1. 比喻（明喻和暗喻）**Analogy (similes and metaphors)**

E.g. This hot spring is like a heaven for travellers. **(Simile 明喻)**

這個溫泉對於旅客來說就像是一個天堂。

Gambling is an evil. **(Metaphor 暗喻)**

賭博是個魔鬼。

2. 誇張 **Hyperbole**

E.g. If we don't cooperate to reduce air pollution, Hong Kong will soon be a dead city.

如果我們不協力減少空氣污染，香港很快就會變成一個死城。

3. 重複 **Repetition**

E.g. Just that simple. You're right, just that simple.

就是這麼簡單。你說得對，就是這麼簡單。

4. 表達肯定的詞彙 **Expressions of certainty**

E.g. I'm sure you'll agree that... 相信你會同意……

Everybody agrees that... 所有人都同意……

No doubt... 毫無疑問……

True, ... 的確，……

3.151 範文 Sample writing

1 Dear Principal, teachers and fellow students,

2 It's my honour here to share with you, my fellow students, some of my thoughts about using smartphones. First of all, let me ask you a question — if you had to live without your smartphone for a day, how would you feel? I'm sure most of you would feel annoyed because you rely so much on your smartphone. True, the smartphone is such a lovely device that provides so many functions for our daily life. Let me first talk about how the smartphone improves the life of teenagers.

在開首以虛構的情況讓聽眾思考和引起他們的興趣。'I'm sure...' 和 'True, ...' 等詞彙可增強說服力和讓演講顯得口語化。

3 A major way in which the smartphone benefits teenagers is definitely the fast information flow. Now, we can know more about current issues on news apps anywhere, as long as there's internet connection. Also, we can watch animated videos on the phone conveniently. With our phone, we can easily know what's happening in the other parts of the world. Other than that, we can get the latest news of our friends as well. Last Saturday, the minute my cousin posted a photo of him with a birthday cake, I realised it was his birthday. I said 'Happy birthday' to him immediately so as to congratulate him. See, how convenient it was!

分享個人經歷，以增加論點的說服力。

Although the smartphone brings us so much convenience, it also brings some problems. Addiction, for example, is one of them. A lot of teenagers spend hours after hours on their phone, and some even hold a smartphone in their hands when they're having a meal. I'm sure most of you have the experience of typing meaningless comments like 'Yeh, cool' on Facebook or Instagram. You skipped your revision as a result. You wasted a lot of time as a result. The attractiveness of the smartphone is just so hard to resist.

以例子加強論點的說服力。此處重複 'You... as a result.' 能突顯花太多時間於智能手機的後果和引起聽眾反思。

4 Although I've talked so much about the nuisance of using the smartphone, in my opinion, it can be a blessing for us if we can manage our time well. If we can control the time we spend on our phone to avoid addiction, we can enjoy the great convenience it brings. But how do we have good self-management? It's just as simple as putting away our phone for just an hour or two when we need to study or do something important. We can all do it, right?

在結尾鼓勵聽眾採取行動，並以反問句突顯行動是容易的。

Thank you for listening, my fellow students. I hope you'll find your smartphone a source of convenience rather than a nuisance.

3.152 體裁小測驗 Quiz

1. 演講開始前，觀眾致意的次序是怎樣的？

2. 演講時，應用疑問句還是反問句引起讀者興趣？

3. 寫演辭時，可用縮略語（contractions），例如 we'll 嗎？

4. 本單元中提及甚麼詞彙可讓演講的語氣更肯定？

答案：

1. 慣常的做法是先提及嘉賓和要員。例如 Secretary for Justice Mr Leung, Dear Principal, teachers and fellow students, ...。

2. 兩者皆可，只是效果不同而已。疑問句可引起讀者思考，反問句則可表達立場或意見。例如，在呼籲人多作慈善捐款的演講中，疑問句 'When was the last time you made a donation to charity?' 可讓人回想起他們何時捐款給慈善機構，從而讓他們思考自己作慈善捐款的次數是否足夠；反問句 'Don't you think the needy deserve more help and attention?' 則清楚表明立場，指出貧窮人士需要更多幫助和關注。

3. 絕對可以。演辭最終是講出來的話，因此所用的句子都應口語化。

4. 'True,...'、'No doubt...'、'Everybody agrees that...' 和 'I'm sure you'll agree that...' 都可讓演講的語氣更肯定。

Unit 4

你也可以試一試 Now it's your turn!

4.1 Write a diary entry

You went to an office building where the electricity suddenly went out. You were trapped there for several hours but ended up meeting some new friends. Write a diary entry about what happened and how you felt.

4.11 範文 Sample writing

1 18th June, 202X Sunny

2 Today I went to the Immigration Department office building in Sheung Wan to apply for a visa to travel abroad. On my way to the entrance I saw the lights flicker — it sent a chill down my spine. However, it was important that I apply for my visa as soon as possible because I had to visit my grandparents in Switzerland. Therefore, I swallowed my fear and stepped into the building.

Things went smoothly and I was amazed by the efficiency of the staff. Yet, the strange cold feeling still didn't leave me. I was terrified when no one else was in the lobby and that I was the only one in the long, dark corridor, but I quickly regained my composure and shrugged off the cold feeling behind my back, telling myself that the staff had just left for their lunch break. Nevertheless, the eerie mechanical sounds caused by the escalators were still very unsettling.

簡短描述所發生的特別事情。

3 By the time I went to the main entrance, I saw five people near it. One was an elderly woman, one was a teenager applying for a visa just like me and the other three were a family who had come to apply for an ID card for their son. They were all decently dressed, considering it was a government office. I was just starting to take a good look at them when suddenly the whole building went dark! The small boy started crying and we all took out our smartphones immediately and turned on the flashlights. Moments later, we were all sitting in a circle, desperately holding our phones as if they were our lifelines.

詳細描述特別的人和事物。

Several hours passed but we still couldn't reach the police because the signals on our phones were too weak. Suddenly, the boy's mother cried out in pain. She was pregnant and her amniotic fluid had just burst! As a medical student, I immediately sprang into action. I helped the lady get into a labour position. After an hour of painful screams and struggles, she delivered a baby girl with my help. At that exact moment, the lights turned back on and we were immediately rescued by firemen. Our five-hour wait was finally over!

詳細描述所發生的特別事情。

4 Tomorrow, I am going to meet May, the mother I helped. Her husband James was very happy about his new child while his son Desmond was very excited about having a sibling. I have also become good friends with William, the teenager applying for a visa. To my surprise, I learnt that his parents live in Switzerland too, and we're planning to travel there together. As for Mary, the old lady, she was very grateful for my quick action and commended me for my bravery. She invited me to have a tea at her house. Today's experience has taught me to remain calm in emergencies, and I hope that I can continue to help others in need. I feel a sense of fulfilment knowing that I made a difference today, and I look forward to new friendships and adventures ahead.

描述一天過後的心情和當天經歷的得着（例如汲取到的經驗或教訓）。

4.2 Write a blog entry

You are the lead singer in a band. Last week, you performed at a music festival in the West Kowloon Cultural District. Write a blog entry about the performance. Describe your feelings, the audience's reactions and the lessons you have learnt.

4.21 範文 Sample writing

1 **Frankie's Music Blog**

2 **Our Band's Debut: A Roller Coaster Performance**

Submitted by Frankie Wong on 28th July, 202X 8:47 p.m.

3 If you've been following this blog for a while, you should know that my band Energy had been planning our first performance. After months of preparation and hard work, our band's debut finally took the stage in West Kowloon Cultural District last Friday. I have to admit that the performance started off as a failure. Yet, thanks to my mates' support, it went much more smoothly and turned out to be a great success.

開首時簡短描述網誌的主題。

4 As soon as we arrived at the stage, our band was already impressed by the preparations of the organising committee. The size of the stage, the brand-new instruments and the number of seats all showed how grand the music festival was. At that time, a professional band was already on the stage, ready to perform their best. I was amazed by the harmony of their rhythms and the vocalist's singing pace. However, their excellent rehearsal made me anxious, as I feared that I could not be as good as they were.

As the music festival started, our band was the first to appear on the stage. We were going to perform two songs. Unlike traditional bands that rely on drums and bass guitars, our band had Peter as the guitarist, Cindy as the violinist and Mary as the pianist. This was probably a new combination for the audience, so what we received were not cheers, but boos. My heart sank when I heard that unwelcoming noise. Therefore, I could not stay calm and kept on trembling. In the first song, 'Pal's Conversation', I had to sing with Mary as if responding to each other's questions. However, due to the pressure I put on myself, I forgot some of the lyrics, leaving some of Mary's 'questions' unanswered. The song thus turned out to be a weird questioning session with a shy boy staying silent. Consequently, the audience thundered with disapproval and urged us to leave.

詳細描述當天發生的事情。

Seeing this, my mates didn't give up. 'Don't worry, Chris. Let's give our best in the last song and have no regrets!' Mary said. 'Yes, you have our full support. We are ONE band!' Peter added. I was blessed that my mates didn't give up and even encouraged me. I thought I couldn't let them down. In the last song 'Friendship Forever', I was thinking about nothing but my mates' support. The song went more and more smoothly, and Peter, Cindy and Mary even sang together. I danced naturally and showed my joy through spontaneous body movements. The audience began to cheer, and some even tapped their feet to our beats. I finally saw delight on the audience's faces! The last song was definitely a great success as we heard screams of 'I love you' at the end!

5 Reflecting on the experience, two key lessons emerged. First, rehearsal is vital to a successful show. It allows bands to calm down and give their best. If we had arrived earlier for a rehearsal, I believe I wouldn't have felt so anxious at the beginning. Second, we should support each other before a show. Appreciation and support are very important as they motivate people. Next time, we should share a few words of encouragement before we hit the stage.

在結尾描述一天過後的心情和當天經歷的得着(例如汲取到的經驗或教訓)。然後,與讀者互動,例如問讀者問題、邀請讀者留言或關注日後的網誌。

I don't know how our next performance will turn out, but I hope that we continue to improve and grow together. If you want to follow our musical journey, stay tuned for more updates. I'll be sharing our experiences in the coming weeks!

4.3 Write a personal email

You are Iris. You moved to Canada last month and started attending a new school. Write a personal email to your friend Joyce, sharing your new life in Canada and describing a special experience you had recently.

To: **From:**

Subject:

4.31 範文 Sample writing

1 To:	joyce88@hotmail.com	From:	iris111@hotmail.com	2
3 Subject:	Exciting news from Canada!			

4 Hey Joyce,

5 I hope you're doing well! I want to share some updates from my new life in Canada since I moved here last month. It's been an amazing experience so far!

在開首，簡單交代電郵的目的。

Introduction 開首

The weather has been quite a change for me. It's really cold, and we've already had a good amount of snow! The landscapes are beautiful, with everything covered in white. It feels like a scene in a Christmas film! I've been enjoying hot chocolate while watching snowflakes fall — definitely a cosy vibe.

I started attending a new school and I joined the drama club there. We recently performed a Christmas play called 'A Christmas Wish'. I played the role of a poor child, which was a meaningful experience for me. The atmosphere during the performance was captivating — the audience loved it, and we received a huge round of applause.

The best part was seeing everyone come together to celebrate. It felt special to be part of a community during this time of year. I enjoyed acting with my new friends, which made me feel more at home.

Matter in detail 內文

I can't wait to tell you more about my adventures in Canada. Let's catch up soon — I'd love to hear what you've been up to!

Conclusion 結尾

6 Take care,

7 Iris

小提示

私人電郵的語氣親切、友善，而且常用縮寫（例如：'I hope you're doing well!'），讓人閱讀起來有與親朋好友說話的感覺。電郵可簡單作結，例如以 'Let's catch up soon.' 或 'I can't wait to hear from you.' 作結。

4.4 Write a letter of advice

You are Dr Chung, a doctor and editor of a health magazine. You have received a letter from a teenager Nicky, who has been smoking for more than five years. He mentions that he wants to quit smoking but finds it very difficult. Write a reply to him, providing some effective suggestions on how to quit smoking. Do not include an address.

Good Health Magazine

______, 202X

Dear ______

4.41 範文 Sample writing

1 23rd March, 202X

2 Dear Nicky,

3 I've read your letter and I totally understand the problems you're facing. I know that quitting smoking can be a hard task. My father was also a smoker. He tried to find an effective way to quit smoking but failed. To help him, I studied this issue for a long time. The methods I came up with helped him quit smoking and improve his health. Therefore, I'm confident that my suggestions will help you.

I'm sorry to hear that you find quitting smoking really hard. Tobacco addiction is really hard to stop, but not impossible. First of all, you should try to smoke fewer and fewer cigarettes each day. My father used to smoke like 20 to 30 cigarettes each day. Yes, that was horrible! I encouraged him to slowly reduce the number of cigarettes by two each week. It took a while but it was effective. This is also a classic method for reducing tobacco addiction. Not only did my father find it effective, but many other people did too. Also, try to distract your hands and mouth so that you won't always want to smoke. You can chew gum to distract your mouth and get a portable game player to distract your hands. My father found those methods very useful and now I can't defeat him in any of the games!

On the other hand, you may consider seeking help from professionals. I believe through anti-smoking workshops, you will learn about the harmful effects of smoking. For my father, when he attended a workshop, the speaker showed some real-life video clips of patients suffering from lung cancer. And that was when he decided to quit smoking.

Lastly, what my father did was go to a rehab centre. I know it sounds like a place you don't want to go to, but my dad was forced by me to go there. At first he found it really hard, but after a while he made friends with others who were also trying to quit smoking. Also, his friends there gave him emotional support and social acceptance. I strongly suggest that you consider this option. It may be tough at the beginning

Introduction
開首

在信件開首點出問題，給予支持和鼓勵。可指出自己或他人的經歷，讓忠告聽起來更有說服力。

清楚指出問題，表達明白對方的感受，然後用 'You should try to'、'You can'、'You may consider' 和 'I strongly suggest that' 等短語忠告對方。

適當使用較口語化的句子可令信件看起來更親切。

Details of your advice
詳細忠告內容

but it'll be worth it in the end. Look at my father now — ten years ago he was lonely and sad, and now he is a really happy man, who has many friends and new hobbies.

Details of your advice
詳細忠告內容

I really hope my suggestions will be helpful for you. I believe that if you follow my advice, you will be able to quit smoking. Remember, it's not an overnight process as it takes time to fully quit smoking. Be strong and do what you need to do, and slowly but surely, things will get better.

Conclusion
結尾

在信件結尾再次給予支持和鼓勵。

4 Best wishes,

5 Dr Chung

4.5 Write a story in the first-person narrative

You are entering a short story writing competition on the topic 'An argument with a friend.' Write a story of about 500 words in the first-person narrative.

小提示

你須以第一人稱寫作故事，以 'I' 稱呼自己。

4.51 範文 Sample writing

1 It was a sunny Sunday morning in May, and the local sports centre was buzzing with excitement. The annual badminton tournament had drawn competitors from all over the region, and my best friend Anthony and I were eager to showcase our skills as a doubles team. We had practiced tirelessly, dreaming of winning the trophy that was shining brightly on the trophy table.

何時 ：A sunny Sunday morning in May
何地 ：The local sports centre
何人 ：Anthony and I
何事 ：Playing doubles in a badminton tournament

2 As we warmed up, the air was filled with laughter. Anthony, always focused and determined, encouraged me while we hit a few practice shots. Our chemistry on the court was strong, built through years of friendship and countless games together. We felt ready for the challenge ahead.

The first few matches went smoothly. We communicated well, scoring points with ease. However, as we faced tougher opponents in the quarter-finals, the pressure began to mount. Our opponents were skilled, and the score remained close. With each lost point, I felt the tension rising, and I started to lose my focus.

During a crucial rally, I misjudged a shot and let the shuttlecock slip past me. Frustrated, I turned to Anthony. 'You should have covered that side better!' I snapped, my voice sharper than intended. His face fell, surprise and hurt mixing in his expression.

關鍵分的誤判引起拍擋之間的爭執，故事引入高潮。

'What do you mean? I was right where I needed to be!' he shot back, his voice rising. The crowd's attention shifted, and I could feel eyes on us as our argument escalated. Each accusation felt like a blow, and soon we were no longer communicating — we were arguing.

3 The argument was at its peak when we lost a critical point because we had stopped paying attention to each other. I slammed my racket down in frustration, and Anthony turned away, his disappointment evident. 'Maybe we shouldn't be playing together,' he muttered, his voice barely above a whisper. My heart sank. I had never meant to hurt him, but my competitive spirit had taken over.

4 Not until that moment did I realise that our friendship was more important than winning. In a moment of calmness, I took a deep breath and turned to Anthony. 'I'm sorry, man,' I said in a sincere voice. 'I shouldn't have blamed you. Let's just play our game.' He looked at me, the anger in his eyes softening as he considered my words.

'I'm sorry too, Edwin,' he replied. 'I didn't mean to lose my temper. Let's work together.' With a renewed sense of teamwork, we refocused on the match. The crowd began to cheer us on again, and quickly we regained our momentum.

在故事的結尾，兩位主角互相道歉，矛盾得以解決，友誼更勝從前。

Although we ultimately lost the match, we walked off the court with our heads held high. Our friendship was intact, and we had learnt a valuable lesson about communication and support. As we left the sports centre that day, I knew that no matter the outcome, our bond would always be stronger than any competition.

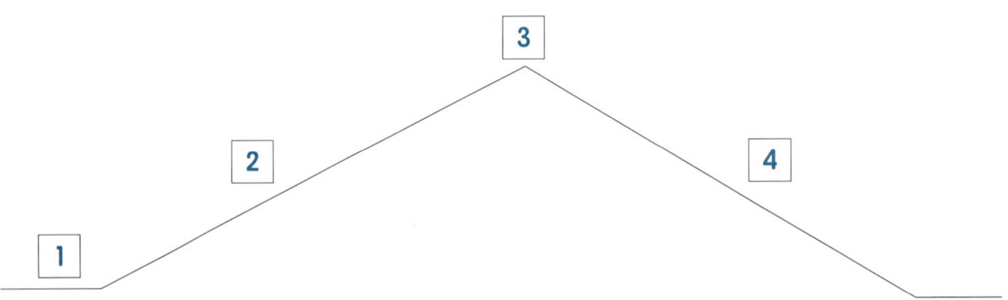

4.6 Write a story based on the pictures

You are entering a story writing competition. Based on the pictures below, write a story of about 300 words.

4.61 範文 Sample writing

1 On a bright Saturday morning, Alex and his younger sister Mia were happily watching their favourite cartoon about clever rabbits. They sat on the sofa, enjoying buttery popcorn and giggling as the rabbits went on silly adventures. Colourful cushions were scattered on the floor, but the siblings were too focused on the cartoon, so they didn't notice them. Everything felt perfect and fun, making it a wonderful way to spend the day together.

> 先描述圖中最明顯的部份，包括兄妹看關於兔子的卡通和吃爆谷。然後，描述圖內其他可見的事物，例如散落在地的坐墊。

2 Suddenly, a loud noise came from the balcony, breaking the happy mood. Alex turned his head, curious about the sound, while Mia kept laughing at the funny rabbits on the screen. Even though Alex felt a little worried, he decided to go to the balcony and check what was happening.

> 先描述圖中最明顯的部份：男孩注意到露台有聲音，但妹妹卻沒有注意到。然後運用想像力創作男孩所想。

3 When he peeked out, Alex's eyes grew wide in shock. A burglar stood there, holding a knife and looking around. Alex wanted to yell, but he covered his mouth immediately as he knew he had to be quiet. He rushed back inside, where Mia was still laughing at the cartoon.

'Quick, Mia! We need to hide!' Alex whispered urgently, grabbing her hand. 'There's a burglar outside! Just follow me!' Alex pulled her towards the wardrobe. They squeezed inside, and Alex quickly took out his smartphone from his pocket. 'I'm calling the police,' he said, his hands shaking slightly as he dialled. 'But first, let's remember the clever rabbits from our cartoon. They often have to hide from sneaky snakes, just like us!'

'Yeah! They always find a way out!' Mia replied, trying to calm down.

'Exactly! If they can do it, so can we,' Alex reassured her. 'We just have to be quiet and wait for help.'

> 先描述圖中最明顯的部份：男孩走到陽台上，看到手裏拿着刀的竊賊。男孩感到震驚，掩着嘴巴。然後，運用想像力創作男孩如何引領妹妹一起躲到衣櫃裏。適當加入對話，例如男孩和妹妹在衣櫃裏的對話，讓故事更生動有趣。

4 They waited in silence, and minutes felt like hours. Suddenly, they heard loud voices outside. 'It's the police!' Alex said, feeling relieved. Then, they heard the front door crash open. Soon after, they heard the burglar being arrested. 'We got him!' one officer called out. A few minutes later, they

peeked out from the wardrobe. The police were there, making sure everyone was safe. 'You're safe now,' an officer said with a smile, and Alex felt grateful. They stepped out, relieved and feeling like the clever rabbits who always found a way to escape danger.

運用想像力創作合理的結局，描述難題如何得以解決。在結局裏，竊賊被警察拘捕，男孩和妹妹安全地走出衣櫃。

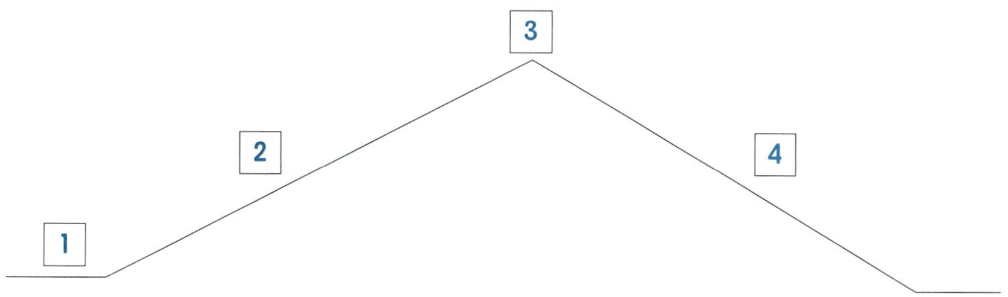

4.7 Write a formal letter

You are Peggy Ma, a student at Sunlight College. You have noticed some environmental problems in the district where you live. Write a letter to the district councillor Ms Audrey Chu, describing the problems and providing solutions.

Dear ________,

4.71 範文 Sample writing

1 5th February, 202X

2 Dear Ms Chu,

3 **Environmental Problems in Our District**

I am writing to raise some environmental concerns in Tsuen Wan that I believe need your attention. My name is Peggy Ma, and I am a student at Sunlight College. These issues affect both the environment and the people here, and I would like to share my thoughts on how we can address them.

Introduction
開首

Firstly, there is too much rubbish in parks, streets and other public places. Many rubbish bins are often full, and some people throw rubbish on the ground, causing hygiene problems. To address this, I suggest adding more bins in public spaces and emptying them more often. We can also start awareness campaigns to teach people about keeping public places clean.

Secondly, the air quality in our district is getting worse, mostly because of vehicles and factories. This is harmful to everyone's health, especially children and the elderly. To improve the air quality, we could encourage people to use bicycles, public transport or electric vehicles. Planting more trees would also help clean the air and make the district greener.

Lastly, the lack of green spaces in Tsuen Wan means that residents do not have enough places to relax and enjoy nature. I recommend creating more parks and community gardens. These spaces would provide a place for families to gather and improve the overall atmosphere of our district.

以 'I'm writing to...' 指出信件的目的，亦可用 'I would like to...' 來指出另一個寫信的目的，例如建議解決方法。

以 'firstly', 'secondly' 和 'lastly' 簡單分段，然後以主旨句點出每段的主旨。

Matter in detail
內文

Thank you for taking the time to read my letter. I hope we can work together to solve these problems and make our district a better place to live. Please let me know if you need more information or help with these ideas.

Conclusion
結尾

在結尾作簡單總結，亦可再次強調問題的嚴重性或建議的重要性。

4 Yours sincerely,

5 *Peggy*

Peggy Ma

Student, Sunlight College

小提示

給予建議時，可用 'we can', 'we could', 'I suggest' 或 'I recommend' 等字眼。

4.8 Write an invitation letter

You are Freddy Cheng, the secretary of the organising committee of Hong Kong Science Innovation Competition. Write a letter to Ms Britney Ma to invite her to attend the Award Presentation Ceremony as she has received a Golden Award.

INVITATION

Dear ,

4.81 範文 Sample writing

1 5th August, 202X

2 Dear Ms Ma,

3 It gives me great pleasure to inform you that you have received a Golden Award in the prestigious Hong Kong Science Innovation Competition for your exceptional project in 202X.

以 'It gives me great pleasure to inform you that' 來告知喜訊。這是邀請函常見的開首。'We are delighted to invite you' 亦是邀請函常用的句式。

We are delighted to invite you to attend the Award Presentation Ceremony, where you will be recognised on stage for your outstanding achievement. You may also invite either your principal or a teacher at your school to celebrate this significant occasion with you.

The Award Presentation Ceremony will be held on 14th August, 202X (Sunday) at 3:30 p.m. in Shatin Town Hall. To indicate your attendance and the name of the accompanying guest, please scan the QR code included in this letter and fill in the information by 13th August, 202X.

清楚交代日期、時間和地點。

清楚交代如何回覆是否出席活動。

Should you have any enquiries, please contact Mr Freddy Wong at 2233 4567. I look forward to honouring your accomplishments at the Award Presentation Ceremony.

以 'I look forward to honouring your accomplishments' 來表達期待見到收件者出席活動。也可以用 'I look forward to celebrating your achievements'。請注意，由於此處 'to' 是介詞 (preposition)，隨後的應為動名詞 (gerund)。

4 Yours sincerely,

5 Freddy

Freddy Cheng

Secretary

Hong Kong Science Innovation Competition

4.9 Write a complaint letter

You are Monica Chiu. You had dinner at Sunshine Restaurant on 6th June, 202X but found the food and service disappointing. Write a complaint letter to the manager of the restaurant, providing details of your visit and demanding a refund for the meal.

, 202X

Dear Manager,

4.91 範文 Sample writing

1 7th June, 202X

2 Dear Manager,

3 I am writing to formally express my dissatisfaction with the food and service I experienced at Sunshine Restaurant on 6th June, 202X. I had high expectations based on the recommendations from review platforms, but my visit was deeply disappointing.

> 在投訴信的開端，清楚指出欲投訴的事項。

Firstly, the quality of the meal was far below acceptable standards. The soup I ordered was too salty, making it impossible to eat. The salad had an unpleasant smell, raising concerns about its freshness. To make things worse, I found a fly on the steak I ordered. This not only ruined my appetite but also made me question the hygiene standards of your kitchen.

> 清楚指出投訴項目，如到餐廳用膳的日期、所點的餐點項目和服務詳情。

When I spoke to the waiter about these problems, he did not seem to care. He told me the food was fine and even said I was being annoying for complaining. Seeking further assistance, I approached the supervisor. Unfortunately, he informed me that he was busy and walked away without addressing my concerns. The responses of the staff were unprofessional, leaving customers ignored and unvalued.

Considering my unsatisfactory experience, I am requesting a full refund for my meal. I believe this is a reasonable request considering the circumstances. I have attached the receipt and photos of the food to support my complaint. If I do not hear from you within the next week, I may consider sharing my experience on social media and review platforms to warn other potential customers.

I look forward to your prompt reply. Should you require any further information, please feel free to contact me at 9876 1234.

> 在結尾留下聯絡資料，讓被投訴的機構容易與你聯絡，並跟進你的投訴。

4 Yours faithfully,

5 *Monica*

Monica Chiu

4.10 Write a film review

You recently watched a kung fu film titled *The Duel at Huashan*. While you thought some main characters performed well in the film, you were disappointed with other elements of the film. Write a film review.

Film Review

THE DUEL AT HUASHAN

4.101 範文 Sample writing

The Duel at Huashan is a kung fu film set in the Ming Dynasty and features a collaboration between Singapore and Hong Kong actors. With a budget exceeding $150 million, the film is backed by Singapore tycoon Chen Yunjian, who also plays a significant role. The story follows Jiang Lei (Charles Ching), who seeks to obtain the legendary Sword of Dragon from the highly respectable kung fu master Zhao Quan (Chen Yunjian). To claim the sword, Jiang Lei must defeat various kung fu masters at Huashan and ultimately be tested by Zhao Quan in the final duel.

可在影評的開首指出電影的背景和電影的類別。

角色的名字後可用括號交代演員的名字。

The film beautifully captures Jiang Lei's journey as he trains in the forests and waterfalls, supported by his devoted girlfriend Xiao Qian (Tian Dandan). Their romantic storyline is touching and adds emotional depth to the narrative. Charles Ching and Tian Dandan delivered commendable performances, showcasing their chemistry and bringing their characters to life. Director Lawrence Yam did a commendable job in guiding the actors and creating an engaging atmosphere, effectively highlighting the film's strengths despite its flaws.

可在內文評論演員的演技和導演的拍攝技巧。

However, the film's enjoyment is significantly marred by the performance of investor Chen Yunjian. His acting skills were lacking, with odd facial expressions and a struggle to execute the fighting scenes, which should be the highlight of any kung fu film. Instead of the dynamic action expected, his movements appeared awkward and forced. As a result, the duel between him and Charles Ching relied heavily on special effects. Instead of showcasing real skill and talent, the excessive reliance on computer-generated imagery made the action sequences feel disconnected from reality.

The cinematography did an excellent job of capturing the beauty of the landscape, which played a significant role in the film's atmosphere. The fight choreography of all actors, except Chen Yunjian, was commendable — the action sequences were well-executed and showcased the martial arts skills of the performers.

除了演員的演技和導演的拍攝技巧，亦可評論電影的其他元素，例如攝影技巧和武術指導。

In conclusion, *The Duel at Huashan* had potential with its strong cast and stunning visuals, but the lack of talent from the investor in both acting and fighting overshadowed these strengths. It would be better for him to focus on investing rather than acting in kung fu films. This film serves as a reminder that not every investor should take on a role in the projects they fund. <u>If you're a fan of kung fu films, you might find some enjoyment in the action, but be prepared for a disappointing performance that might spoil the experience.</u>

在結尾對電影的評價作總結。對於好壞參半的電影，可簡短總結其可取和不足之處。

4.11 Write an informative text

Write an informative text about the Great Wall of China. There should be at least six subheadings, including 'Introduction', 'History', 'Construction', 'Summary' and two other subheadings of your choice.

The Great Wall of China

Introduction

History

Construction

Summary

4.111 範文 Sample writing

可用小標題組織文章，讓讀者清楚知道每部份講述的內容。

資訊性文章是正式文體，故須避免使用縮寫。

The Great Wall of China

Introduction

The Great Wall of China is an iconic symbol of Chinese history, culture, and engineering. It is also a famous tourist attraction.

History

The Great Wall was primarily built during the Warring States Period (475–221 BC). Qin Shi Huang ordered its expansion during the Qin Dynasty (221–206 BC) to unify the walls of different states. Various dynasties contributed to its expansion, with the most well-known sections constructed during the Ming Dynasty (1368–1644).

Construction

The Great Wall stretches over 13,000 miles and is made from various materials, including earth, wood, bricks and stone. Its design features watchtowers and fortresses for military observation.

Purpose

Originally, the Great Wall served as a defence against northern invasions. It also helped facilitate trade along the Silk Road and controlled immigration and emigration.

Restoration Efforts

Over the years, significant restoration projects have been undertaken to preserve the Great Wall. These efforts aim to maintain its condition and cultural value, ensuring that it remains a symbol of national pride.

Summary

The Great Wall of China is not just an architectural marvel — it shows the strength and creativity of the Chinese people. Taking care of the Great Wall allows future generations to understand its importance and history.

4.12 Write a proposal

You are a member of the organising committee for the Mid-Autumn Festival celebration at Wisdom Garden. Write a proposal to the management committee of Wisdom Garden, outlining the activities that could be organised for that night.

Proposal for Activities at Mid-Autumn Festival at Wisdom Garden

Introduction

___

___

___

Recommendations

___

___

___

___

___

___

___

___

___

___

___

Recommendations

Conclusion

4.121 範文 Sample writing

1 **Proposal for Activities at Mid-Autumn Festival at Wisdom Garden**

2 **Introduction**

As a member of the organising committee for the Mid-Autumn Festival celebration at Wisdom Garden, I am pleased to present a proposal for activities that could enhance the celebration and foster community spirit. The Mid-Autumn Festival is a cherished occasion, and our goal is to create an enjoyable evening for residents and their families.

在開首清楚指出計劃書的目的。

3 **Recommendations**

(a) Lantern Display and Competition

在建議的部份加入小標題，可讓讀者清楚知道每項建議的主題。此外，每段以主旨句先作交代，然後給予詳細內容。

We propose to organise a lantern display, where residents can contribute their handmade lanterns. This would not only beautify the surroundings but also encourage creativity among participants. A lantern competition could be held, with categories for the most traditional, the most creative and the best in show, offering supermarket coupons to winners.

(b) Mooncake Tasting

To celebrate the flavours of the Mid-Autumn Festival, we suggest a mooncake tasting event. Local bakers could be invited to showcase their mooncakes, allowing residents to sample various flavours. This event could also include a workshop on how to make traditional mooncakes, providing a hands-on experience for participants.

(c) Cultural Performances

We recommend incorporating cultural performances, such as traditional Chinese dance, music and storytelling. These performances could highlight the significance of the Mid-Autumn Festival and engage the audience. By inviting local schools or cultural groups, we can foster a sense of community involvement.

4 Conclusion

We believe that these activities will create a vibrant and memorable Mid-Autumn Festival at Wisdom Garden. By promoting creativity, food appreciation and cultural enrichment, we can strengthen community bonds and ensure that this celebration is enjoyed by all. We hope our proposal will be considered favourably, and we look forward to your feedback. Thank you for your attention.

在總結裏，禮貌地請求讀者採納建議和給予意見。

4.13 Write a survey report

You are a student in 2C. Your class conducted a survey about 'the favourite transport of 2C students'. Based on the survey results below, write a survey report and provide reasons for some of the findings.

Findings of the Favourite Transport of 2C Students

Total number of students: 40

Transport	Number of students who like the transport	Number of students who take the transport to school
Taxi	20	2
MTR	10	25
Bus	8	8
Minibus	2	5

Survey Report on the Favourite Mode of Transport of 2C Students

Introduction

____

____

____

____

____

Survey results

Conclusion

4.131 範文 Sample writing

1 **Survey Report on the Favourite Mode of Transport of 2C Students**

2 **Introduction**

A survey on the favourite mode of transport of 2C students was conducted during a lesson last week. A total of 40 students were asked to indicate their preferred mode of transport and whether they use it to travel to school.

在開首指出意見調查的問題、對象和人數。

3 **Survey results**

The survey results indicate that the most popular transport among 2C students is the taxi, with 20 students expressing a preference for it. However, only 2 students reported using a taxi to get to school. This may be because taxis are often seen as a more expensive option, and many students prefer cheaper ways to travel.

描述調查結果時，可先描述數字較大的項目，然後順數字由大至小描述其他項目。

The MTR is the second most favoured transport, with 10 students liking it. Notably, a large number — 25 students — take the MTR to school. This is likely because the school is conveniently located near Kwun Tong MTR Station, making it an easy choice for many students.

The bus is preferred by 8 students, and it is also used by 8 students to get to school, indicating that those who like this mode of transport also use it regularly. Conversely, only 2 students prefer the minibus, with 5 students taking it to school.

4 **Conclusion**

The survey results show that while many students like taxis, very few use them to travel to school because they can be expensive. In contrast, the MTR is liked by some students, but many take it because it is close to the school. Overall, the findings highlight different transport choices among the class.

在總結中，可簡略重提數字最大和最小的兩項。

4.14 Write an argumentative essay

Nowadays, many people undergo cosmetic surgery to enhance their appearance. However, there are potential problems associated with these procedures. Write an argumentative essay stating your views on cosmetic surgery and supporting them with reasons.

4.141 範文 Sample writing

1 **Cosmetic Surgery: More Harm Than Good**

> 標題清晰表明立場。除了 'More Harm Than Good'，也可以用 'More Drawbacks Than Advantages' 或 'More Negative Effects Than Positive'。

2 Nowadays, many people choose cosmetic surgery to enhance their appearance. While some argue that these procedures can boost confidence, I believe that cosmetic surgery brings more adverse impacts than helpful outcomes. The risks and emotional effects of these surgeries often outweigh any short-term benefits.

> 在開首提供背景資料，指出爭議出現的原因。然後，用 'I believe' 來表明立場。

First, there are significant risks involved with cosmetic surgery. Any surgery can lead to problems like infections and scarring. For example, procedures like liposuction and breast implants can sometimes lead to serious health issues. Many people do not fully understand these risks, thinking only about how they want to look. This can lead to dangerous situations that could have been avoided.

Moreover, the emotional effects of cosmetic surgery can be negative. Many people seek surgery because they feel insecure about their appearance. However, even after surgery, they might not feel better about themselves. Studies show that some individuals develop an unhealthy focus on their looks, worrying about flaws that others do not even notice. Instead of helping people feel good, cosmetic surgery can make them feel worse.

> 以簡單的主旨句點出段落的中心思想，然後擴展。

> 提供最少兩個理據以支持你的立場。

While some may argue that cosmetic surgery can improve self-esteem and help individuals feel more attractive, this view overlooks the deeper issues involved. True confidence comes from accepting oneself, not from changing one's appearance. There are many ways to boost self-esteem without surgery, such as engaging in hobbies that bring joy. These alternatives can lead to lasting happiness without the risks associated with surgery.

> 指出反方意見，然後反駁。

3 In conclusion, while cosmetic surgery may seem like a quick fix to improve appearance, the dangers and psychological effects may exceed the advantages. It is essential to focus on self-acceptance and celebrate our unique qualities instead of relying on surgery to feel good about ourselves.

> 在結尾重申立場和總結論點，可以用 'To conclude' 或 'In conclusion' 作總結。可比較議題的益處和壞處（或優點和缺點），說明作出取態的原因。如指出缺點比優點多，亦可用 'The potential harms may be greater than the benefits.'

4.15 Write a speech

You are the chairperson of the Environment Club at your school. As the opening of the Environmental Protection Week, the principal has asked you to give a speech about 'Bring Your Own Bag'. Talk about the importance of bringing one's own shopping bag and how this will reduce plastic waste.
Director of Environmental Protection is a guest of honour.

Dear Principal, teachers and fellow students,

4.151 範文 Sample writing

1 Dear Principal, teachers and fellow students,

2 As we kick off Environmental Protection Week today, I want to talk about something that can make a real difference in our life and our environment: 'Bring Your Own Bag.' You know, it's not a catchy slogan; it's a call to action! Did you know that globally, we produce over 300 million tonnes of plastic every year? A significant portion of this ends up in our oceans, harming marine life and disrupting ecosystems. The simple act of bringing your own shopping bag can have a profound impact on this crisis.

這句在激發聽眾的意識。通過對比，講者能更有力地傳達出環保的緊迫性和必要性。

開首直接陳述演講的主題，同時以令人震驚的事實引起聽眾興趣。

3 Let me share a quick personal story. Last month, I went shopping in Mong Kok, and I forgot my reusable bag. I ended up buying a few items and was handed one of those flimsy plastic bags. As I walked home, I couldn't shake off the feeling that I was contributing to a problem that's so easily avoidable. It felt like carrying a weight I didn't need!

個人經歷能夠引起共鳴，使聽眾更容易理解和接受演講者所傳達的信息，也能使演講變得更生動有趣，吸引聽眾的注意力，並激發他們的思考和行動。

Now, let's think about plastic waste for a moment. In Hong Kong, we use around 10 million plastic bags every day! That's shocking, right? Imagine if we all just decided to bring our own bags instead. It'd be like turning off the tap while brushing your teeth — you're saving water without even thinking about it. Every little action counts!

So, why bring your own bag? First, it cuts down on the mountains of plastic that end up in our landfill sites and oceans. You don't want to be part of the problem, do you? Act now! Each time you shop, make it a habit to grab your reusable bag. It's simple, and it shows that you care.

反問句能引導聽眾反思，不僅強化了聽眾的責任感，還激發他們的內在動機去改變。祈使句傳達了一種緊迫感，鼓勵聽眾立刻作出改變。

And here's a thought: how many times have you seen a plastic bag blowing in the wind, floating aimlessly like a discarded balloon? It's a sad sight, and it reminds us that our choices have consequences. If we all took a moment to think about where our waste goes, we'd probably make different choices.

此問題能引起聽眾的共鳴和反思，使聽眾回想自己的經歷。此外，通過將塑膠袋比作被遺棄的氣球，演講者使聽眾更容易理解塑膠袋的無序漂浮所帶來的負面影響，從而促進他們對於保護環境的重視。

As we can see, bringing your own bag isn't just about convenience; it's about making a statement. It shows that you're committed to a cleaner, greener Hong Kong. Plus, it

使用縮略語，例如 'isn't'、'it's' 和 'you're'，讓演講聽起來口語化，更簡潔易明。

can even save you money! Many shops offer discounts if you bring your own bag. So, you'll be doing good for the planet and your wallet!

4 Don't hesitate! Let's take this opportunity to inspire each other. Talk to your friends and family about using reusable bags. Share tips on how to remember to bring them. Maybe you can even personalise your bags to make them your own!

So, let's bring our own bags, reduce plastic waste, and create a brighter future for our beautiful city. Thank you.

在結尾鼓勵聽眾採取行動。祈使句能傳達出強烈的行動呼籲，鼓勵聽眾主動參與環保行動，並與他人分享這個理念。

這種語氣能夠激發聽眾的積極性，讓他們感受到自己在這個過程中的重要性。此外，通過具體的建議，如與家人朋友交流和個性化袋子，演講者提供了可行的步驟，使聽眾更容易付諸實踐，從而促進整體的行動意識。

分析文中這個段落分別用了甚麼演辭的技巧。

(a) 數據 A figure	(b) 明喻 A simile	(c) 行動號召 A call to action
(d) 反問句 A rhetorical question	(e) 虛構的情境 A hypothetical situation	

Now, let's think about plastic waste for a moment. [1]In Hong Kong, we use around 10 million plastic bags every day! [2]That's shocking, right? [3]Imagine if we all just decided to bring our own bags instead. [4]It'd be like turning off the tap while brushing your teeth — you're saving water without even thinking about it. [5]Every little action counts!

答案：

1. (a) 數據 A figure

   通過提供一個震驚的數據，演講者能強調問題的嚴重性，並促使聽眾反思自身的行為，並了解改變的必要性。

2. (d) 反問句 A rhetorical question

   吸引聽眾的參與，鼓勵他們反思所提供的信息。反問句促進了共同的關注和認同感，使聽眾感到自己參與了討論，而不是被動的聆聽者。

3. (e) 虛構的情境 A hypothetical situation

   幫助聽眾在心中構建一個理想的畫面，並激發他們的想像力。通過描繪一個積極的未來場景，演講者能讓聽眾感受到改變的可能性，並激勵他們思考如何參與這個改變。

4. (b) 明喻 A simile

   使抽象的概念變得具體和易於理解。通過將與日常生活中的熟悉行為進行比較，演講者展示了小而有意識的選擇如何帶來顯著的環保效益。

5. (c) 行動號召 A call to action

   鼓勵聽眾採取具體行動。通過強調每個人的努力都是有意義的，演講者能提升聽眾的參與感，讓他們意識到即使是微小的改變也能產生累積的效果，從而促進更大的環保行動。

強化詞彙 Elevate your vocabulary

Fill in the blanks with the correct words from the box below. Each word can be used ONCE only.

Passage 1

thrilled	amused	bored	annoyed
hopeful	terrified	confident	nervous

Last Saturday, I was **1** ________ to go to the amusement park with my friends. I had been waiting for this day for weeks! However, when we arrived, the lines were so long. I started to feel **2** ________ because I had nothing to do while waiting in the line for the roller coaster.

After waiting for an hour, I became **3** ________ and said, 'Let's do something else. I hate waiting in lines!' However, my friend Sarah remained **4** ________ and said, 'I think we'll get on the roller coaster soon!'

Five minutes later, we finally got on the roller coaster. At the beginning, I was **5** ________ that I would not scream on the ride. 'There's nothing to be afraid of!' I said. However, as the roller coaster was going on a steep slope, I started to feel a bit **6** ________. Finally, I screamed a lot and even cried during the ride. I was really **7** ________ of the heights and high speed!

After the roller coaster ride, my friends and I watched a performance of clowns. It was really funny and we were all **8** ________ by the clowns' silly acts! Then, we played some booth games and bought some souvenirs.

Today was really an interesting day because I got to spend time with my friends. I hope to meet them again soon!

答案：

1. thrilled	2. bored	3. annoyed	4. hopeful
5. confident	6. nervous	7. terrified	8. amused

Passage 2

disappointed	inattentive	over the moon	dissatisfied
scared	excited	irate	worried

Good afternoon, everyone! Today is a special day, and I feel so 1 ________ to be standing here in front of you. As I look at all of my classmates, I am 2 ________ to see how far we have come together.

However, I must admit that there were times when I felt 3 ________ about my grades in exams. There were also moments when our teachers felt 4 ________ because we let them down. Some of us were 5 ________ in class and missed important information. Some of us were so naughty that we even disrupted the class. Our teachers were 6 ________ that they had to shout at us. Fortunately, we all learnt a lesson from our wrongdoings.

Today, we should focus on the positive. Let's celebrate the achievements we've made. If you're 7 ________ with what you've achieved, work harder for your dreams. Also, don't be 8 ________ of difficulty and challenges as they are opportunities for growth and learning. Be prepared and stay focused on your goals, and remember that every setback is a step towards success.

Thank you!

答案：

1. excited	2. over the moon	3. worried	4. disappointed
5. inattentive	6. irate	7. dissatisfied	8. scared

Passage 3

petrified	sleepy	hesitant	furious
impatient	heartbroken	relaxed	at a loss

It was a typical Tuesday morning and the bank was uncrowded as usual. The tellers were 1 ________ as they knew that they did not have to deal with many customers. The security guard was 2 ________ and wanted to take a nap. Suddenly, the door burst open, and a masked figure with a gun entered, causing everyone to feel 3 ________.

The robber shouted demands, but a customer, Mr Smith, was 4 ________ and shouted at the robber, asking him to leave immediately. However, his anger made the situation worse. The robber shot him twice and some ladies screamed. The bank manager was 5 ________ and unsure of what to do, but he tried his very best to stay calm. He told a teller to get cash out immediately. The teller was a bit 6 ________ at the beginning as she paused for a moment. Despite her fear, she knew she had to follow the manager's order so as to avoid more shooting.

As the teller was getting cash out, the robber seemed to be very 7 ________. He glanced at his watch several times and was about to lose his temper. He even pointed his gun at different customers.

Before the situation got worse, the police arrived and arrested the robber. Mr Smith was sent to hospital immediately but was pronounced dead. The staff and other customers were safe but they were all 8 ________ when they heard about Mr Smith's death.

1. relaxed	2. sleepy	3. petrified	4. furious
5. at a loss	6. hesitant	7. impatient	8. heartbroken